Sex Goblin

Sex Goblin
by Lauren Cook

Nightboat Books
New York

ISBN: 978-1-643-62233-0

Author photo by Dallas Houston

Design and typesetting by Rissa Hochberger
Typeset in Neue Haas Grotesk

Cataloging-in-publication data is available from
the Library of Congress

Nightboat Books
New York
www.nightboat.org

for Dallas

If I had a recital of sorts
If it was important to me and I asked you to
come, would you come?
Would you drive. 2, 3 — no, 4 hours? Would you
drive 4 hours to come see me play?

When we went on a field trip to the butterfly conservatory everyone wanted the butterflies to land on them. Of course this was nearly impossible. Nobody I went with and nobody who was trying to could get a butterfly to even come near them. There was only one person who made butterfly contact when I was there. It was an older woman with three butterflies on her head. The people working there said her hair mousse attracted the butterflies and they were sucking on it. They wouldn't let her leave though until the butterflies left her hair on their own accord because it was strictly against policy to touch them. Nobody was allowed to stop the butterflies from eating, or shoo them away. So the woman waited and complained. She sat on a bench and complained about wanting to go home because she had butterflies on her head eating her mousse off her hair and she wasn't allowed to touch them.

There's two singular one dollar bills in the grass
I walk by everyday with my dog. I take him there
to go to the bathroom in the morning. I haven't
picked them up because I'm scared they are
laced with something like acid or fentanyl which
I read about on Facebook in my mom's group.
I leave them. Someone else can get drugged
through their skin. Four days later there is only
one bill left. I noticed one was gone and the
other was covered in the morning frost. I wonder
if the person who took one got drugged like I
suspected. I won't pick it up because it is a test I
think but I also wonder if i'm doing the right thing.
Like maybe I'm not open enough to accept the
wealth flowing to me. But I know it's a death trap.
I know it in my heart.

My dad sends me a text message that says
"Everyone wants to be something else. It's so
sad. Musicians want to be actors, actors want
to be rock stars. Politicians are failed celebrities
because they are ugly and have no talent
By and large."

My mother can't see because she lost her glasses. So she is sort of disabled currently in a sense, because her vision is so bad that she is essentially bed bound. She can see about four inches in front of her face, nothing in front or behind. When she looks at her phone it is four inches from her face. Before I leave she asks me to come as close as I can to her so she can look at me. I hold my face four inches from her and watch her eyes focus and she smiles and says she loves me and that I look very beautiful.

i am a man of no personal taste or opinions really.
I will have whatever: I always tell people, hey man!
I'm easy! Haha! Yea, i'll eat whatever. Clothes are
just clothes you kno? As long as they're comfy
I don't mind too much how they look. I just don't
think about it. I drink but not too much. I've smoked
cigarettes before but I can't remember the last
time I had one. I love all the furniture in my apartment and my shoes and my bed. They all work
for me. You wanna meet at the park? Ok I will go
there. You wanna go to the mall? Sounds good to
me too. We can go to Europe or an island maybe.
I don't know much about either but it seems to be
where vacations occur.

U have to trust that the person editing the film
knows what to look for in the raw footage
I'm not one to brag except when I brag

can't lie to ya can't lie without you

The convincing comes from a place of deep sadness

This is technically the most beautiful world we will
ever get

Sex goblin I decided I don't hate you anymore

If you can forget what iconography means anything
is possible
Sex goblin used to not let themself do things
because they had a hard time forgetting what
everything meant

Sex goblin forgot that having fun means forgetting
what things mean and then making new meanings
Sex goblin learned how to enjoy things
Sex goblin's New Year's resolution was to say yes
to life

Sex goblin knows feelings are results of conditions
not forever
Sex goblin just waits the six hours for their bad mood
to turn back into a regular mood

Sex goblin likes being haunted
Sex goblin doesn't get uncomfortable

Sex goblin makes other people happy first and last
Sex goblin knows the answer to every riddle
Sex goblin can only listen to music with words in it

This guy I was dating once . . . every time there was a bug he would ask me to put it in a cup and take it outside. I'd be like, "Ok. I can do that." I kind of assumed he was scared of bugs or something, or felt I was better equipped at it. I was ok with this role. I am the one who deals with bugs. One day his roommate knocked on the door and said, "There is a bug in my bathroom. Can you help me get it out?" He sprung up and was like, "Yea for sure!" and ran right into her bathroom and put the bug in a cup and took it outside. I was like, "What the fuck? I thought you were scared of bugs? You always ask me to take the bugs outside?" He said something like, "Oh well I don't know . . . I just always felt like you liked doing it so I let you do it. I let it be your purpose." This made me upset.

We all make mistakes and talk about it with each other and try to figure it out and when we see each other, when the people who make mistakes that affect each other see each other, we try to make the best of it and just try to smile and laugh and give each other another try because that is all that can be done.

We both said "If you're happy I'm happy" to each other and then no one could decide if we were happy or not or whose opinion would be in charge anyway if one of us were to be unhappy.

Well, I reckon I know even less than you
On account of the fact that I've never seen a
horse before
Never led one to water
Never even had to go to the water on my own before
So . . .

It would be fun to write a story about someone who can't remember their own life, and they feel incredibly haunted and compelled to search and figure out what their life means and to understand and know all the things that have happened to them and why. This makes the main character feel very alone and isolated. They look at all the people around them and they wonder why everyone has it so easy. The people around them don't seem to think about these things. The character thinks to themselves, "Everyone around me is happy because they can remember their lives." The main character is always unhappy, and can never be present, because of their obsessive fascination with how different they are. Their obsession with how no one understands the mission they are on. At the end of the story the main character finally learns that nobody else can remember their lives. Not a single person. They don't understand a single thing that has happened to them either. But they just decided to let it go and try to be happy and enjoy each other's company. All the other characters then ask the main character why he never wanted to hang out more. They say, "We always tried to get you to hang out . . ."

I actually don't know if it is that hard to be able to tell if someone likes you. You can usually just tell because of how long they look at you.

I want everything to feel like I'm reading it on a bathroom wall

I collect many things. I have collections of many things. I collect marbles, tiny angel figurines, dolls, salt and pepper shakers, stuffed animals, Hot Wheels, posters, movies, CDs, records, tapes, tour memorabilia, commemorative t-shirts, unopened vintage candy, all types of trading and playing cards, and so on and so forth. I collect so many things though and I am interested in so many things, that I can only have one of each category. I don't have enough storage in my one bedroom apartment. So as you can see, I have a very large collection, but only one of each thing from each collection. I have ONE baseball card. I have ONE antique porcelain doll. I have ONE patch from a National Park. I have ONE coin. Together they make up a collection collection.

In my dream last night I was a beautiful brunette female celebrity. I wasn't famous in the dream but I had her body and face. I got a haircut and went to the Hermès store and bought a leather choker. I remember opening the orange box, taking it out of the dust bag, and wearing it out. I was running my beautiful fingers all over my soft new hair like it was a horse's tail.

I felt beautiful in the store. When I left the store and walked down the street people yelled at me and told me I was ugly and I didn't feel beautiful anymore. The Hermès choker was thick and had metal chainmail hanging from the bottom that went down my neck and over my clavicle. I was wearing some type of corset or something because I couldn't help but stand up straight. Someone tried to grab the choker off my neck to embarrass me and make me feel small but they couldn't.

About a year ago, I decided I wanted to adopt a dog. We watched the humane society's website for weeks, looking at new dog listings, until we saw a cute pug mix. We went to the humane society to meet a dog named Snuggles. He was part pug, part something else that I have no idea. Grey and wiry with big eyes and some visible skin. He was so ugly he was beautiful and I loved him. We filled out the paperwork. Sadly though, the lady said that someone else had already filed the paperwork and that they will probably get approved but we will be pre-approved next time for the next dog we want. And if their paperwork didn't go through for some reason we would get Snuggles. I was sad. Being on the waiting list meant we did not get the dog. I go home.

I opened up Grindr. A man named Richard has messaged me. In his picture he is holding Snuggles. It is this man shirtless, holding the dog I just met at the humane society and wanted but wouldn't be able to adopt.

He says, "Hi."

I said, "Is that Snuggles?"

He says yes. "It is Snuggles. How do you know?"

I said, "I just met him today at the humane society."

Richard says, "My mom made me give him up

but he is a cuddle bug and a love bug. I hope you get him."

I said, "Me too but I don't think I will."

Richard says, "What are you doing later?"

I say, "Nothing. Goodbye."

We obviously did not get Snuggles but also Richard kept messaging me semi-consistently with no response until I left the area to move somewhere else.

Another day and the man who is the main character in the story wakes up still full of anger.
Anger is a runaway truck ramp that shoots up
and off the highway, to keep you from going
down the mountain. Anger keeps you from feeling and moving through shame. The man takes
the ramp off the highway everyday because
he feels incapable of going down the mountain, even though it would just momentarily be
uncomfortable. Everyday though he drives the
truck up the anger ramp instead of going down
the mountain because he is so scared of the
way it will feel to go down. But avoiding it everyday, it's actually a lot more work.

I differ from my roommates because I like hearing
the man who lives upstairs cum

There are no more four-leaf clovers. They have officially been declared "extinct" as their place on the endangered species list has been established since 2035. Nobody thought of four leaf clovers as entirely separate species until the leading work of clover scientists innovated the field in 2025. A hunch of one doctorate student drew many more to follow suit, and examine more closely the knowledge we have always taken for granted. By looking at the DNA more closely, it has gone beyond thought that it is your run-of-the-mill mutation or mistaken gene expression. The four-leaf clover evolved separately, with there being an advantageous trait in having four leafs instead of three. This has established it as an entirely different subspecies. These four leaves allow them to photosynthesize better. This is true for all types of clovers. Both those in the Trifolium genus and the Oxalis genus. Scientists have named both species *Trifolium lucky* and *Oxalis lucky*.

The reason four leaf clovers have remained so elusive is their inability to reproduce and carry on their traits. They are often poached for human enjoyment. Their seeds can not come to fruition to carry on their genes. This is what allowed people to always credit this anomaly to mutation, but their rarity stemmed from eugenics. Loss of habitat.

I tell myself I'm not writing about love anymore unless it is somehow imperative to describing something else: an experience, a place I was, a time.

If my hair is all messed up you know I've been in my dungeon just thinking and pulling on it

If the moon can be half-full and half-empty then so can the glass. The glass waxes and wanes!!!!

The guy at the deli said what does your hand tattoo say?
I said true love. He said do you believe that?
I said not so much anymore but I don't think about it.
He said well I definitely believe in making love. I said right on boss. Have a good day.

I always used to be like, "Do you think there will be an encore?" Like, the thought of not knowing if there would be an encore made me anxious. Now, I just keep remembering my friend turning to me and saying "If they don't turn the lights on immediately at the end there's probably gonna be an encore."

Two summers ago for some reason everyone within a few weeks decided to tell me that
they've kissed their cousins. I don't remember
who was the first person to come out to me and
say that or how it was brought up. Someone was
talking about how their first crush was on their
cousin when they were like five to seven years
old, which I could understand because who else
do you know? But then they told me they used to
practice kissing on their cousin. As small children
them and their cousin would kiss. I considered
this person to be really normal and well-adjusted,
not like that really means anything but I don't
know, so I was really surprised.

Cuz I consider myself not normal I guess and
I had never kissed any of my cousins. I figured
someone who I thought of as well-adjusted would
not have kissed their cousin and I also figured
if I was as depraved as I thought I was I would
have kissed my cousin. My main point though, is
that what makes me different from this person
is that if I did kiss my cousin I would probably
never ever ever tell anyone about it. I was mostly
taken aback by this person's openness they dis-
played when telling me they kissed their cousin. I
thought you kept stuff like that secret.

A few days later and someone else tells me their first kiss was with their cousin. For the next few weeks I asked everyone, "Have you ever kissed your cousin?" and a lot of people said yes. I think I liked hearing about it because I liked listening to everyone tell me something I would have literally never considered telling anyone if it happened to me.

The more I think about it the more I think it reflects a lot about me and what I was taught that I think it's weirder to tell someone about kissing your cousin than it is to kiss your cousin at all. It doesn't have to be about kissing your cousin obviously. But in general, what makes me not normal here is more so the inclination to believe that if I kissed my cousin I could tell no one because no one would understand me or love me if they knew I kissed my cousin. Meanwhile a lot of people are kissing their cousins I guess. And everyone was there for each other.

my thoughts are my Bible I don't even question them at all and I'm always right

On the train over the city you can see the magnolia blossoms the size of someone's head. The
magnolia trees leave these blossoms for the
tops, for the insects and birds above. Outside
our apartment one blossomed at street level.
It was like a rose cabbage. Smelling the flower
makes me feel like I just took a shower. The next
day I come outside to smoke a cigarette and
the flower has been cut clean off the tree with a
sharp knife and taken.

Best part of being in a relationship is always
knowing who to buy gifts for

I just mixed up the word confetti and crouton but
there's something in that

Everything now is about getting over fear

Imagine a rolled up overlapping string, similar to how we store our headphones in our pockets or extension cords in boxes. This cord only has to cross over itself three times in order to have the whole thing turn into one large knot. This has been studied by physicists, who also calculated the percent probability of headphone cords getting tangled based on their length. I told my friend I read about this and a month later he texted me saying, "I know you are only into knots lately but did you know it is only possible for a human to fold a paper in half seven times maximum?"

The woman before me in line said "I only came here for butter. I just ended up picking up so much other stuff."

The Aldi cashier says, "Don't worry I do that too."

He asked me if I wanted my receipt and my brain lagged for a second and I said, "Yes, sorry, it took me a second to understand what you said."

He said, "Don't worry I do that too."

I think he just sits here all day and tells people "Don't worry. I do that too."

The man from the story is always conscious that he could leave one day, to go to work, to get on a plane, to walk to the store just to pick something up, and could never come back. He knows you never know what's gonna happen. Because of this, he has a great fear of leaving things unsaid. He does not want to die on the way to work and have the last thing he said to his family not be what he would want to say on his deathbed. When he fights with people and they are about to go to sleep angry he says, "I actually have a thing against going to sleep angry. It is somewhat a compulsion. In case I die in my sleep I need you to know I love you and I am not angry. And if I don't wake up tomorrow dead I still find it incredibly beneficial to reiterate my love for you and I stand by what I say."

One time in an Uber on my way home from work me and the driver drove past the waste treatment plant below the on-ramp and she pointed at it and said to me, "have you heard about the poop factory accident?" and I of course had not and she said "well I guess a while ago this father and son were flying in a helicopter over the city and their helicopter crashed into the poop factory and instead of dying on impact they drowned in the poop." and I said wow what a tragedy and she said yes, so tragic. Anyway I tried to Google it and I don't think that happened. I tried all sorts of combinations of the words "helicopter" and "treat-ment" and "plant" and "Bay Area" and "Crash".

Having a lover is making a quilt out of many small
closed-door rituals
until the blanket is so big you can sleep under it
every night
and if you don't want to sleep under it you leave.
Simple as that

Today I met two people who know how to ask questions
I met them and said hi how are you and they said
good how are you and I said good and instead of
then sitting in silence they said so, where are you
from? Pretty crazy, right??

Lately I've been thinking about how much easier it would be for me to talk if I had the gift to sing instead. Some people just sing and I do not. I talk and although I think I have good things to say I think you could say anything if it has a good tune. I think when you talk there is nothing carrying the words. Really just accepting someone saying something requires more suspension of disbelief than enjoying a song.

You can actually walk pretty damn well over a
burning bridge
Doesn't even matter that it's on fire

If you ever can't stand the smell of fermented,
rotting food when you're taking out the trash
just imagine it's the alcohol breath of someone
you're in love with!

The other day I told my friends from Los Angeles about the first time I was in Los Angeles. My LA friend took us to Santa Monica and we watched the sunset over the water. I had never seen that before. In New York, at Jones Beach and Coney Island the sun always sets on the opposite side of the ocean. You see the sun set over the boardwalk at the end of a perfect day. In cartoons and postcards, the sun always sets over the ocean. My friends tell me they've never thought about that before.

Five months later in the car with whatever boyfriend was there at the time, I tell him this story. I tell him about how the sun sets over the ocean here. I said I never got to see the sun set over the ocean before I got to California as an adult. He says to me, "Well, I've never seen the sun *rise* over the ocean. In New York that means you get to see the sun *rise* over the ocean."

The flower is not the brain of a plant or something. The flower is a reproductive structure
that comes to fruition when the plant has stored
enough energy & has reached that point in its
lifecycle. The flower's purpose is to become
fertilized by whoever's job that is and to produce
its fruit, which is a blanket term for its seed and
whatever flesh or container the plant produces to
hold and spread that seed.

And then after it flowers the plant dies and its
hope is placed on the carrying and spreading and
germinating of its seeds or it is a plant that does
not die every cycle and its leaves die back and
it lives underground for the winter for sometime
and comes back each year until it dies of natural
causes or whatever.

So the flower is not the brain but some plants live
for seventeen years before they can get enough
energy to flower and if you picked that flower
they would never be able to heal and never be
able to produce a flower again or another leaf
and die. And there are other flowers where it is
good to pick handfuls.

There's something in the physical nature of a lot of animals where we can not be controlled around sugar and/or alcohol (maybe some other consumables) and that is what actually makes me feel the most connected to being alive and a species on the planet. I love nectar also. It defines my relationship to life, and it serves no purpose beyond me. The animal's life is marked with inherent unwavering purpose because its need for sugar is connected to an important biological function which is the pollination of flowers. There is no equivalent under capitalism for us really to participate in webs like this, in America, as there is a severing between us and the biological functions we could or should be performing (seed dispersal, pollination, other aspects of stewarding) as we meet our own needs (this is the model used by all other living things). For example, the bat seeking a flower at night flies right into the hand of a scientist to photograph it. The main commonality I see worth focusing on is flying into the scientist's gloved hand because you need nectar so bad. Who else flies into the gloved hand every night just to get high??? Hm???

One time when me and one of my exes were taking a shower together in some house we were staying in and she watched me pick up a face wash and put a huge dollop in my hand and wash my face with it. She said to me, "whose face wash is that?" and I said, "honestly I have no idea" and she said, "well you sure as hell used an awful lot for not knowing whose it is!"

I think about this time like seven years ago when someone I was dating complimented me by telling me they loved my "big beady eyes" and my "crooked cartoon teeth." I think about it all the time, but lately I've been thinking I need to learn to let go of some of the things I heard people say to me over and over again in my head for years if I just listen to new people talk for a second . . . it's not even like when the day ends and I ask god for gifts I ask for straight teeth and eyes that don't resemble beads. I don't care about having those things. It's more so like, holy shit seven years ago someone said something to me that vaguely hurt me at the time but now I consider it to be like a movie and I'm in the mood to watch it considering how formative it was.

When I fly over a city I'm convinced the football fields are only there for scale.

Sometimes when your enemy is invisible it either
means you're facing the biggest enemy of all time
or you have no enemy at all and I think that's why
things get so mixed up and confusing sometimes

I wasn't here for the rain but I can see the slick
on the road
And it smells like rain
So therefore there was rain

Peter is homeschooled. He is in eighth grade.
Next year, after summer when he is finally in high
school, he gets to go to public school. It is what
he pushed for. What he asked for. And because
his mother believed so much in young adults
having autonomy, she agreed. Peter is very smart.
He loves to read. Loves researching, loves nature.
Loves the natural world. Loves being outside.
Fishing, hunting, tracking, hiking, foraging, bot-
any, herping . . . he loves it all. Peter's mother
taught him a lot about that, gave him the tools
he needed to learn so much. They had land, and
time. Peter could pursue any project he wanted.
He was interested in following scat and tracks to
find animal dens. He liked mapping topographi-
cal areas of forested land. Because of his beliefs
about recycling and using all of the parts of animals (some people call this nose-to-tail eating)
he enjoyed collecting roadkill. Naturally, in line
with all of his other hobbies, he enjoyed tanning
and skinning hides. The best way to practice is
on fresh animals, the kind every other driver just
passes. Peter goes and collects these animals.
He takes them home and wears gloves and uses
a sharp knife and slits the animal from under
its chin down and along the legs and arms and

peels the hide off like a sock inside out. He then egg-tans them after salt-drying them. It's a rough finish, but it's what is accessible to young Peter. Peter naturally collects many hides, and because of his willingness to master any craft (and time from lack of social interaction) he decides to take up pattern-making and reading, as well as sewing, so he can make a suit out of the furs.

Peter finds a book on suit patterns. He makes a suit pattern. Peter finds an old sewing table and machine in one of the barns. Makes it work, oils the parts, cleans it. Peter finishes his beautiful fur suit. It has tones of gray, caramel and amber colored browns, black, white . . . it is gorgeous. A work of art. A testament to what humans are capable of. An honor and salute to the natural world. Peter's mother is proud of him. Everyone is proud of him because he worked hard at something. He got good at it, and accomplished his goals and saw them through.

On the first day of ninth grade Peter is nervous. He wants to wear his suit. Peter's mother suggests he doesn't. She is a hippie, but she is not delusional. She is grounded and aware of the reality that although Peter wants school, he might be really taken aback by how much it contrasts with how his life has been so far. The life she provided for him. Peter is offended that his mother says this. He wears regular clothes though, and when he gets to school he changes into his fur suit.

At first he feels very confident. He sees himself in the bathroom mirror and he is very happy. He smiles at himself. He leaves the bathroom, goes into the hall, and faces drop. His new peers are disgusted. Eyes hit the floor. People point, laugh, gawk. Every bad reaction you can name. Peter didn't know. Peter knew about the bus and lockers and other things like that but he didn't know people would not like his fur suit? People begin screaming at him. And then, in a way nobody could really imagine it escalating, a book is thrown at Peter's head. It came from someone in a crowd. Really there was no way to know who exactly. Another book was thrown from another side of the crowd. That's all it takes. People began throwing things at Peter. He turned and went to run and the only choice was back into the bathroom. He was cornered, such an epicenter of attention that a circle had formed around him. Someone yells, "Freak," someone yells, "Faggot." These thoughts are racing through his head while he's being plummeted/pummeled with objects, Nobody even knows who he is. They don't know his name, they just don't like his suit. They are scared and confused so they hurt him.

Little tasks

Mark of the beast
A sign on the side of the road that says
PUSSYWILLOWS

I still take the long way home on purpose in order
to kill as much time possible before I have to sit in
an empty house

So, goblin,
You forgot to take care of yourself again
You forgot to prepare again
You got halfway here and already want to turn
around again.

I can just tell one day my bath is going to fall through the ceiling. How do I know? A woman always knows, they say.

I can feel it. I still fill the tub with warm water. I sprinkle epsom salt into the bottom for my muscles. Sometimes I put in a few drops of an essential oil. Usually historically lavender but right now I'm into frankincense and sometimes cedarwood too because they are such clean scents but also warm and musky. Old timey and religious feeling.

The tub is cold though. I heat the water to the hottest it can be but the tub is cold. My landlord told me it is because the tub is not insulated underneath, and it sits above our two-car garage which is not insulated either. So the warmth radiates off the bottom and goes down to the garage. And the cold air hits the bottom of the bath and blows the warmth away. So the bath is always kind of cold.

And I know it is going to slip through the floor. When I sit in it and close my eyes I can see and hear the wind blowing on it. It's just a few creaks away from collapsing. I can feel it

Anyway it did one day. I was not there though. My cousin from out of town was staying at my place.

I was staying at my boyfriend's. Recently I got a new boyfriend, not to brag. But she was staying at my place because she was here for a work convention type summit thing. I'm not sure, I can't keep her story straight. She didn't even end up going to her work obligation until the third day on account of the ceiling falling.

She wasn't in the tub though, when it fell. Which was not part of my vision. I always imagined myself falling with it, inside of it, eyes closed. Very cinematic.

She said she was laying in bed around 3 p.m., midday lull in energy you know – she had just gotten in around 8 a.m. that morning and ran some errands and was ironing and getting ready for the next day. And she heard a loud crash and rip and other alarming noises and knew it was coming from the bathroom and where the tub once was was a large dark hole. And she could see through to the bottom floor, to the garage, and the tub was laying there like it had been there all along and all the pieces of drywall art-fully arranged around it.

I know because she sent me a photo which I sent to my landlord. My landlord did not say it was my fault which was nice, and although it was not my fault it felt like it was. Because I had been thinking about it every day since I got there so naturally I have no choice but to think I made it happen, with my mind and such. Now I can feel the breeze through my whole house.

My cousin got a motel afterwards, for the rest of the weekend. Why would you want to prepare for a conference in a war zone? I kept staying at my boyfriend's house. Thank God for Boyfriends. My landlord will come fix it soon. I'm not worried. I wonder what I will think about now? Maybe I will close my eyes and collapse everything else that stands. When it happens I can say "I knew the whole time"

I write these down because they are all the things I want to tell myself. I am putting them here because maybe someone else wants to read them. They are about me though. I wrote them specifically about my life. I make stuff up, but it's a metaphor for my life or something. It still makes it centered around me though; my wants and needs. You are welcome to read it too and you are welcome to take the pieces that make sense. But we are not the same. I am not right nor offering truth. I am simply taking notes and cataloging experience. We all mostly experience the range of emotions. I am just articulating in the way that makes sense to me.

There's something I want my lover to understand.
I always want to hear what you have to say. I
always enjoy listening to what you have to say.
Maybe I haven't made that clear lately because
you don't feel like I've been listening or because
I talk a lot normally anyway. But, if you think you
want to tell me something I'd love to hear it. I
know I make fun of everything. So, I think you get
scared I'm going to make fun of you. But I'd never
really make fun of you. If I thought you were stupid and annoying, we wouldn't be here.

This "Doomsday Preppers" husband and wife
team have this secret emergency spot they meet
in if they're separated when the world ends and
it's the first place they ever kissed . . .

Fears:
Demons getting to me
Being in a bathtub when it falls through a ceiling
Being hurt while walking down the street
Someone i love killing me in shame
Heights

Things i learned to like that i never liked before:
Vacuuming
Forgiveness
Techno
Sharing food

**i make a list of things to ask you, things i forget
to ask you in the moment:**
Do you have cousins
Where do you want to travel next
What's your ideal party situation
Favorite smells
Do you watch porn

If I'm dying give me CPR
Cuddles
Pets
Rubs

Thomas is not my personal trainer. My personal trainer was a man named Mark, I met with him twice. The first time was fairly normal. He had me run and do various other things to assess my body. I felt adequately pushed. We didn't really connect intensely though. Sometimes something like that is just always off between you and one person. The instant you start talking to them you can see their eyes glaze over. They aren't, like, smitten and instantly taken aback by the energy you're putting off. To be fair though, I didn't feel that about Mark either. My eyes glazed over too. There was a vague indescribable aspect to both of us that both of us found to be immediately off-putting about each other the moment we laid eyes on each other. Nevertheless, we co-existed until we mutually decided to stop scheduling. I still use aspects of the routine he taught me.

I meet Thomas because he is the client Mark met with before me. Upon first arriving I tell the girl at the desk I'm here for a training session with Mark. She says ok I will tell him you're here. He is with another client right now because he really schedules the sessions back-to-back. She says, go change in the locker room and by the time you're done he will be ready. I say ok, cool. I go to the locker room. I change. I am leaning on my locker, scrolling through my phone, looking at the pictures of my friend Janet's baby. I'm happy for her. It is 2:59. I suppose it is time to go out there and meet Mark. Suddenly a very beautiful, tall man walks in the locker room. Sometimes when I am in the locker room I am scared residually. I am scared because I do not want to accidentally make anyone uncomfortable. I do not do anything to make anyone uncomfortable on purpose but I think sometimes when I'm in there people can tell I'm gay and that makes them not even want to stand near me. I get it I suppose. I get it in the sense that it's just a material part of my existence and I've learned to adapt to it. Thomas walks right up to me, puts his water bottle on the bench and begins to open a locker a few down from mine. He is very sweaty, shining from his forehead down and his hair is pushed back with the sweat he just accumulated. He is wearing a ribbed white tank top that he has completely soaked through in the center of the back and chest with a pair of black Nike athletic shorts. He is wearing some running shoes I don't recognize but look like they cost a lot of money. He turns his head and says, "Hi" with a big smile that doesn't feel unwarranted and body language that feels very warm. I say "Hi" back. My eyes adjust downward, I can see his dark nipples through the wet, clinging fabric. I look at the clock. It is now 3:01. I gotta go train now.

I go to the gym and I meet with Mark. The session is fine, I go to the locker room, I shower and change and go home. That is it. I schedule again to meet with Mark the following Tuesday at 3 p.m. I say ok. I like the gym now for some reason . . . I wonder why?

It is the following week. Basically the same situation. I go to the desk and tell the girl to tell Mark that I'm here. I go to the locker room. It is 2:59. I am leaning on the locker sort of waiting I suppose. Thomas walks in. I say hi first this time. He says hi back. I say hi this is my name. He says hi my name is Thomas. I say do you come here every week at this time? He says yes I meet with a personal trainer from 2 p.m. to 3 p.m. I say oh, that's so interesting and crazy! I meet with a personal trainer from 3 p.m. to 4 p.m. He says who? I say Mark! He says me too! I say wow!! Crazy!! I'm stupid so I say some dumb shit like, oh it doesn't really even look like you need a personal trainer. You're so buff already. He laughs and looks at me and asks me what that even means? What does it mean to "need" a personal trainer? I wouldn't think anyone really needs a personal trainer per-se? He's smiling though and I can tell by his voice he's making fun of me seriously but it is to engage me more and make me more interested. I blush, I think. We both laugh. Whatever. He says I'll stay around until 4 if you want. I say what do you mean? He says don't you wanna hang out? I'm taken aback but I laugh and say yes, yes. You're very observant, yes I do. I could kill Mark with my bare hands at this point. Fuck this training session. I go to the gym floor to lift weights. I come back at 4. Thomas is fully showered, dressed, and clothed. He looks just as good clean. I've never seen him not sweaty before. He's never seen me sweaty before. I'm sweaty. I have to shower, I say to him. He says ok. I get in the shower and he sits on the bench right outside the shower and we talk about our lives while I'm in there. He asks me where I work. He asks me where I grew up. When did I move here? Do I like it here? I ask him all the same things.

I take the bus to the gym. I realize Thomas drives a car. He offers me a ride home because it is cold. I get out of the shower and dress in front of him. He doesn't really look but he also does at the same time if that makes sense. I don't care. We leave together. It has taken me so long to shower that it is dark now. This time of year it gets dark early. We sit in his car. I can't tell cars apart. I don't know the make or model of the car. Just that it is shiny and black and has a screen that tells you so much information and the seats and leather with seat warmers and it smells nice in the car. We are in the back left-hand side of the parking lot. I can feel my ass being warmed by the seat and the heat is on full blast but not making hot air yet and I'm shaking slightly because I'm so fucking cold. My hair is wet. Thomas notices and reaches his hand towards my back and starts rubbing the back of my winter jacket. It feels so good it makes me want to cry. Sometimes someone touches your back and it feels like the hand of everyone you always wanted to touch your back. I think of all the times I stayed up wishing I had the warm touch of a hand on my back to make me feel like everything was ok. I can't even recall a single time I ever felt my father's hand on my back to comfort me.

Thomas has full lips, a clean mouth, clean teeth, and a soft tongue. He does not push or pull too hard. He lets me lead his mouth with my mouth first so he knows what I'm comfortable with then he starts to control my mouth. I can't help but let out a little moan. He laughs. We are in the gym parking lot in the dark with the heat on and I am not scared of Thomas. I want Thomas to take care of me. I want to cry because I feel so alone all the time and this surge of excitement is almost too much for my head. My whole body feels hot and tingly like how it feels when I'm mad except this feeling is good this time. I feel like I can't contain this feeling though, so it scares me. I am in a rolling boil. We kiss for a long time before I decide to take Thomas's cock in my hand. I have my hand on his thigh near his knee for awhile, moving my hand until I start to make my way up towards his groin area. For the first time, I feel his body adjust to me. I feel him squirm. I feel him unable to contain something. Cool. The playing field feels finally equal. I work my way up his day clothes, the tailored suit trousers he put on after his gym clothes. I touch his button, I touch the fly. I pretend for a while almost like I cannot notice his dick getting really hard while we kiss. I pretend as if my hand is simply resting there by accident. Peripherally though, I can tell his cock is huge. Even with just half of my hand slightly resting on it I can tell it is larger than average. This is the largest cock I've ever even been near! This novelty excites me. Any novelty really excites me, so I finally unbutton and unzip his pants. He is wearing boxer briefs. Makes sense. He smells and feels clean. His pubes are trimmed but not shaved. I find that courteous and realistic. I push his cock through the flap in his underwear while making eye contact with him. There felt like there was no noise, no passing of time for a minute. I hold his cock in my hand and think about how my hand feels in comparison to his cock size. I'm like haha, look at my hand for scale! In Thomas's mind I think everything I was doing was just coming across as building the suspense. That is, until I decide to finally throw my entire mouth over his sex. I first put the head of his penis in my mouth, then the whole thing, bobbing on it for a while and playing with his balls. Even though it is so large it feels kind of easy to put inside me fully because I feel relaxed and at ease and I like challenges in general. At first, Thomas does not touch me. He lets me bob on his cock and honestly I could not tell if he even liked it or not. He didn't make a noise. I could not tell if he was just letting me do this because he felt like it was a nice thing to do for me. Halfway through though, I finally feel his large, strong hand on the back of my head forcing his cock deeper and deeper into the back of my throat. Thomas seemed like an apprehensive participant until he started fucking my face. I'm not going to lie, it kind of hurt. I liked how it hurt though. I liked how it felt like I couldn't really breathe. I knew that if I said no Thomas would stop. After a few minutes, Thomas cums in my mouth. Thomas cums like he hasn't cum in awhile. It is a large load with a very specific taste and he moves a lot and makes a lot of noise when he finally ejaculates. It takes him a long time to ejaculate too. His voice cracked as he managed to get the words "I'm cumming" from in between his lips. He rams the cum to the back of my throat, and I don't let go of my mouth's grip on him until he kicks me off his cock. After he cums his penis sits throbbing in my mouth for a moment while I suck everything out of it. I massage the last drops of pleasure out of it. I swallow his cum. He withdraws and sighs.

For a second there is silence. I assume I am going home now. Thomas breathes for a while. He buttons his pants. He has his eyes closed then open finally when he seems to have returned to earth. Thomas says nothing, he just reaches now for my cock. He does not act with hesitation. He directly goes to my cock, feels that it is hard, unbuttons my pants and reaches for it and puts it in his mouth. Almost in one continuous motion this happens. As it is happening I feel unable to process it. The most surprising part to this all seems really just to be that Thomas wants to suck my dick back. Not sure if I just have low expectations though. Thomas is larger than me in every way. It is easy for him to put my cock in his mouth. He puts the entire thing in his mouth and immediately starts sucking with intense and vigorous passion. I reach again for Thomas's cock, which I am now in love with (the cock, not Thomas, although I like Thomas), and he does not pull away. I put my other hand on the back of his head and now I fuck his face. I feel his cock go from completely flaccid to hard in my hand while I ram myself inside him. I feel like it has been maybe thirty seconds honestly before I can not take it anymore. I am going to cum!! I cum in Thomas's mouth. I would never cum anywhere else, not in a nice car like this with a nice interior. Not when

I'm a guest! I feel the release, I feel Thomas suck harder when he feels my cum flooding his throat. I am feeling very frenzied at this point, and then immediately after my climax I feel my entire body flush with warmth. Thomas holds my cock like how I held his in my mouth after he cummed, and he massages it with his tongue until he is sure I'm done. After he disengages, I button my pants back. We sit for a second. He puts his mouth on my mouth again. He tells me I'm very beautiful. I tell him the same. He asks where I live and if he can take me home now. I say yes. He asks if I want to hang out again and I say yes. Maybe I can feel his large cock in my hand again plus he has a car and other nice things. I still see him sometimes. About every other week. He takes me to dinner or something then we suck each other's cocks in his nice, warm car. I'm not sure what we will do in the summer.

Tamara opens her front-facing camera, opens Instagram, takes a deep breath, and hits the "live" button

"Guys, I'm sorry . . . I'm gonna let some people trickle in . . ."
There is a pause for about forty-five seconds as the viewers climb from single digit to thousands, as people join her livestream.
I know I'm usually happy. I know I try to spread positivity with my page and be who I wanna see in the world but I don't feel good today. I don't like who I am and I don't like my life and I don't have the energy today to pretend for you guys."
Tamara waits nervously for their responses
Hundreds of comments start flooding in
"Don't worry tamara we love you"
"Tamara i love u for who u are"
"Tamara you don't have to be anyone else"

Oops, for a second there I almost forgot about my agony

My quiet night
I want to protect you and I want you to protect me
Waiting for my delusions to pick me up because
I'm gonna ride them all the way home

Predicting the future is often times not even a beneficial power for the protagonist to have

Lots of different ways to be lovesick. Too much lovesick. Not enough lovesick. Absence of lovesick. Unrequited lovesick. Codependent lovesick. Absolute sick with bliss. Guess where I'm at right now.
I love failure right now, I'm obsessed.

Note to self: before you start immediately counting on your fingers just try to do the math in your head first.

The strongest spider fiber is made by *Caerostris darwini* aka the Darwin's bark spider. I don't know why the spider was named after Darwin other than the obvious reasons. In reality it is completely arbitrary who gets to name these things. The Darwin spider is an orb weaver spider that was "discovered" in 2009 in Madagascar. I think "discovered" in this sense, like most senses historically, means added to the Western taxonomy. The Darwin spider's silk is supposedly the toughest biological material ever studied. Everyone is obsessed with it because the fiber is ten times stronger than Kevlar which is what they use to make bulletproof vests. Darwin spiders are thought to have evolved to make these webs because they live in riparian areas. Darwin spiders produce the longest bridge lines ever recorded, which they use to cross rivers. Scientists I think originally assumed this biological niche was also to catch large predators but Darwin spiders in general produce wide and sparser webs, and despite their strong silk, this allows large prey caught in their webs to escape usually. Darwin spiders do not make the packed and dense webs needed to retain a very large piece of prey.

Male Darwin spiders engage in oral sex (this essentially means they salivate on female spiders' genitals occasionally) which is incredibly rare behavior to witness in anything but a mammal.

Also the only reason I looked up spider silk anyway is because I was looking at genetic engineering lab kits online and one of them said you can genetically engineer yeast to grow spider silk. Scientists I guess are obsessed with trying to engineer a synthetic spider web. They gave a group of goats genes so that the spider protein would come out with their goat milk when milked but the silk scientists spun with that milk was not good compared to what spiders make in terms of strength.

The scientists eventually figured out that yeast and E. coli can grow spider silk, which eliminates having to milk the spider goats altogether. I think somewhere people even genetically engineered silk moth caterpillars to produce spider silk. I think though, as of finally right now, synthetic spider silks are pretty good and supposedly some are supposed to hit the market soon.

Certain female spiders of various assorted species will form a mating plug in their vaginas. This is when a slurry of spider chemicals and oftentimes pieces of castrated genitals from the male spider that were ripped off are used to seal up the female spider's genitals, like a tampon, in order to ensure that the sperm will not be lost.

Congratulations nobody makes me feel bad like
you make me feel bad
What would you like to do with that news?

Just chillin' at home
Sitting at my desk on my laptop like a monk
before the printing press was invented
Just copying the Bible word for word and when
you finish you just start another one

You ever look God in the eyes and be like I would
do anything to have my pain transformed into any
other emotion. I would do anything to have my
pain replaced by any other feeling. And god says
ok do it then? And you said I don't know how that's
why I came to ask you and god says lmaooo you
definitely know how and you've done it many times
before don't you remember and you're like oh yea

Sitting like a bird rotting in its nest

I can't help you if you don't use your words

As a little kid I loved being like "can you tuck me in before bed?"

Google contacted me to tell me stop googling "swollen lymph nodes" every day . . . they said I was annoying them

I'm not looking for reality

I'm looking for a simulation of reality and I'm not afraid to admit it. Everything is unbearable to look at in front of me. I have had a hard life and a hard childhood so I have to just sit on my phone all day and do many drugs including numbing myself completely with marijuana and other things and sort of eating these foods that make you have diarrhea only. That type of way of living for a long time. So I'll kinda look for an artifice to hold on to anywhere. Whatever is easiest at that time my brain will sort of think up or engage with to make me away from here.

I found an online game where you are a migrating bird. It is the end of winter so you are flying back up north. Leaving Mexico to go somewhere very north, maybe in the Arctic Circle. You do that long flight journey for the first half of the game, non-stop. Over oceans and land along the coasts. It all centers around these sort of made up lands and countries I suppose. It looks geographically like a combination of everywhere, like a drawing in a science textbook they use to show you different land masses (peninsula, plateau, valley, mountains.) Some birds in real life fly up to 500 hours at a time straight across oceans to migrate so it is somewhat based on reality, your long journey over the sea and coast. After you migrate, you mate and sit on eggs and feed the small bird children. You're not any specific bird species though. The animation is these sort of very shiny looking rounded cartoons. I am sure it is for a fetishist of sorts, that its selling point is that, but for me I find it to be accurate enough to suspend my disbelief. But I'm just looking to be anything else. I will move on to the next one soon.

I play Solitaire, Tetris. All the normal games too.

There's another game where you are riding a motorcycle on a rocky woodland path. There is no music and you're being chased by a giant rock that's rolling, sort of one of those cartoon ones from like Indiana Jones. The game is basically *Temple Run* with the giant rock trope. And you're on an enduro motor bike, from the early seventies or eighties. But you're a woman in a bikini with no shoes. And in your basket, which is attached to your bike, are groceries and there is no explanation as to why you are being chased at all or in the bikini. But you still collect coins and jump over obstacles and make sharp turns. It all just seems routine almost and when you finally make it home at the end of the game/across the finish line, the rock just goes away as you enter your front door. There is no celebration or acknowledgement of who, what, when, where, or why. You just start cooking dinner after you bring the bags in.

People who talk shit about "low-hanging fruit"
have never had a strawberry

I can't live a single day more without a birdfeeder

There's this other phone game I saw an ad for
on another phone game I play where you run
a restaurant and have to cook for your hungry
customers. You are very old for some reason,
I think that's the point of the game. It's called
GRANDPACHEF I think people come to the
restaurant because they're impressed with your
ability to be so old and run that kitchen yourself. Anyway nobody helps you. When someone
orders a burger you have to run to each station
and press the button to put the meat on, the
button to take it off when it's done (the timer tells
you when it is done, it can get burnt if you don't
take it off.) You add the cheese with the cheese
button. You have to get the bun and go over to
the toppings bar and click the button to get all
the toppings. You have to put it together. Don't
even forget to drop the fries in the fryer when
you start the burger so they're done together.
Anyway I run that restaurant as an old man, but it
isn't my favorite gig.

There is a video of a man on Youtube cutting a large picture into his field. It is shot from above. I know about the man because the video opens with him explaining what he's going to do and why. He's going to mow a large web in the grass. The web is not for Halloween, no. He is looking to catch something incredibly large, something as large as the size of the field. When he is done it looks good, sort of like really a natural rendition, of quality. He is serious about catching it, whatever it is. There is no game here. I just get invested.

Candy Crush is just Bejeweled. There are soooo many games like that. Have you ever played Bejeweled? Where you get a few of a kind together and you double click and then they explode and give you money and the little things restack to make new combinations and unlock new money. I play one where they're all different types of rocks. And when they explode they are geodes of all different kinds and they look real through the phone. And sometimes when you get it really good there is lava, a crack where it is red inside you can see the center of the Earth and the game helps you see this with a lot of intensity so I appreciate that. A game can take you anywhere.

I had a dream the other night. My first dream in a long time because I smoke so much weed. It is hard for dreams to come through to me to have their messages received. I was a club owner. I ran a nightclub and did everything I could to keep it afloat and provide for the people who needed and wanted the space. I spent much time walking up and down the long corridors in the dark trying to check on different things. At the end of the night something bad happens to the club, as I lock the door it either lights on fire or disappears or blows up or collapses but I feel a deep sense that it is gone in an irreparable way. I can't seem to do anything but focus on how much it feels to have something here today and gone tomorrow, without so much as even a mention. I know I'm only having this dream because of all the phone games.

The worst part is I'm not even like "nobody understands me"
The problem is everyone understands me and they're over it

Nobody's "perfect day" is as follows. Nobody wakes up early. Not so early that the sun hasn't risen yet, but early enough to feel good and like the day is full of possibility. Nobody will take a shower, brush her teeth, do her hair, makeup, get dressed, and go on a walk somewhere outside. She will listen to music while doing these things, including the walk. She will walk in a park or on a short, flat, loop trail that is easy to navigate and not too much time or energy. It is mostly about being outside and starting the day right. She will then go somewhere after the walk and get a nice breakfast, two pancakes with bacon and one egg over. She will have a cup of decaf coffee with one cream and one Splenda packet.

Nobody will come home. She will watch TV and clean her house. She will also listen to music while doing this. Somehow there is new dirt everywhere everyday. It keeps us all busy. Nobody will take an afternoon nap like a cat in the sun. On this day there is nothing else left to do but relax and unwind. Nobody didn't have work the day before and didn't have work the day after. She will wake up in a few hours and prepare dinner of some nice seasonal vegetables and a protein of her choice, maybe also with some bread and butter that is soft and spreadable. She will enjoy a nice light, fruity glass of wine that has been slightly chilled. She will have whatever dessert she wants. And she will not think too much about her name and what that means for her.

I'm gonna see you in my dreams and there's nothing you can do about it!!!

Kirsten is a softball player. She plays adult minor league softball. She squats all day so her thighs are thick and she likes to run and wear loose athletic clothes if she isn't in the uniform so nobody really knows what her body looks like. But I do. Kirsten is 6'2" and I am 5'8" which is tall for a girl but Kirsten is very tall. She makes me feel very safe.

I met her because I was writing an article for the local paper I work for about the minor league stadium changing its grass into fake grass. They were going to make the grass into astroturf. I never really go to the bottom of it per se, and the story got scrapped anyway. Also, they never even ended up doing the astroturf anyway because people started protesting it because someone shared an article on Facebook about how astroturf causes cancer. I think it was a stupid idea solely because the grass was fine and not even that hard to take care of to begin with. We don't live somewhere with droughts, so there's no issue. Water the grass. The day we met, I had just gone into the offices to meet with some managers to ask them questions. I honestly don't really remember much of what we conversed about. They showed me some numbers and graphs that had

projections from the stadium's projected wealth
over a five year plan. I remember being tired and
dehydrated because my eyes were having a hard
time feeling like they could stay awake. I was
bored. They told me when we were done meeting that I was free to walk around and peruse the
stadium. I was like cool, what a free way to spend
my now open afternoon. I didn't want to go back
to the office and it was a warm day. The sun was
out and it was spring. I ran into Kirsten. I at first
saw her from very far away, while overlooking the
field from the benches. She was moving across
the grass and into her position where she squat-
ted and did what a catcher does. I'm still not really
sure honestly at all about the intricacies of it but
it seems irrelevant. They were practicing or whatever. I watched and then waited in the parking
lot after they were done. It took awhile but I had
a book and my phone and water and there were
bathrooms at the stadium obviously so all my
needs were met. I just walked right up to her and
said hi. She said hi back. It was ok and it made
sense. I assumed she was part of lesbian royalty.
To be an adult, lesbian softball catcher.

   The first time we hung out I went to her
apartment. I think it was very clear from the

beginning what we were both doing. Sometimes you don't have to talk about anything or worry about anything. She told me I looked nice in the color I was wearing. In retrospect, I don't remember what I was wearing that night. I said thank you and believed it. We drank one bottle of wine and she kissed me. I was ready. Everything in life in my experience is about adjusting to the set of conditions that have been presented to you. Under the rules of these conditions, under the scientific rules of Kirsten's house, I was the one who was going to take it. But also, that's kinda what I came here for. I like it when someone's hand can cover my entire pussy. There isn't even much time to wonder how or why. What is happening?. It's just happening. We are in her room and she has soft, silk sheets. The type of sheets a bachelor would have and she is most certainly a bachelor. We are kissing and feeling and she has my pussy pressed against her thigh, rubbing up and down. We kissed for a long time. I know better than to touch her because I know she doesn't want to be touched, at least not the first time. In my experience it can take a second for a top dyke to get used to you like that. In reality though, it turns out most gay people can't prescribe to any sets of rules or dichotomies consistently even when they'd made it a facet of their identity (I think people have been historically fighting against these dichotomies but the top vs bottom argument feels so good and kills so much time) and when they do it is often for show. You know Kirsten tells the world she is a top and is a top to the world. I'm not here to argue that, I just also know most people also want to be fucked every once in a while. I don't know how but I ended up on my stomach, sort of on all fours. She had two fingers inside me, thrusting in and out using her hips to push the fingers. I remember looking around and thinking to myself she had, like, eight empty, dirty cups on her dresser that all had to be washed.

In the middle of the night walking next to the freeway
It's so quiet that one car sounds like thunder barreling
Rarely down, one every five minutes or so
Not a lot for a city of millions
Meanwhile all day many lanes operate and I don't
hear it too much

My dog pisses on the floor and there is no one to tell
No one is home

Sex goblin, you think you do not deserve nice things
so you hide in your room

There was a guy pulled over on the side of the road with his flashers on that was holding traffic and it was just because he wanted to take a picture of the way the sun looked on the mountains over the bridge. Fucking dickhead

We don't have to ride or die we can just chill

Have good dreams or none at all love you goodnight

The human brain didn't evolve to perceive truth
It evolved to survive the most effectively
They are not the same thing

Unfortunately for the world I learned that it is now
important for me to keep my best thoughts to myself

Sex goblin I ask you to know your limits
I think sometimes you stick around either from
being used to the pain or because it's something
to do or because conflict is still not boredom and
anything is better than boredom

Sex goblin vaguely feels and knows there was a
time sex goblin was smarter and better or something and thinks of that time as the best time but
actually sex goblin has no way to measure that
tangibly and didn't used to be smarter or better
and there was no best time

In fourth grade we would sit in a circle and read a book. We would take turns reading. Everyone would read a paragraph. When I wasn't read-ing I would hold the book up, over my face, and pick my nose and eat it. I thought because the book was covering my face completely and you couldn't see me literally picking my nose and eating it that nobody knew. Now I realize if my hand is up there and you see movement from the visible parts of my arm and my book seems to purposefully be covering my face, what else could I possibly be doing?

When it's 11:11 and you wish for true love and world peace like a loser

God told me I can't be mean anymore so now I have nothing to say

My customer service skills allowed me to often skirt rules to make difficult customers happy. Depending on the account or retail customer, you play different parts. It's like acting. I know I can apply these skills to a career change. Selling a $24,000 watch over the phone (sight unseen) took skills.

FLOWERS ARE AWESOME . . . I'm a gardener by trade and I like to hike fish be outdoors. But I love a good snuggle movie day also just sort of exploring and looking for adventure! If you have a bike let's go riding . . . like something with an engine not a bicycle. I have a thing with lame ass jokes the lamer the better. Hit me with your worst joke and let's get this party started!!

The opposite of two ships passing in the night is two ships in a head-on collision. It doesn't matter what time of day

There was once a very bad and scary man. He would go around and find all the four-leaf clovers and rip the fourth leaf off of them. This would turn the clover back into a regular three-leaf clover, thus rendering the clover's magic wishing powers useless.

One day he was punished. He met a witch in the woods. The witch was an old and wise woman who minded her business and practiced her magic outside of the village for many years. He had wandered to the edgelands, and the witch had witnessed him pulling the fourth clover leaf off four-leaf clovers she had planted specifically because this is an ingredient in common magic spells and things like that. The witch in that instant had thought that was a crime of great proportions, very selfish and mean, and to make the man learn she turned him into a pair of underwear. The witch had never showered or changed her underwear before.

She took off her underwear, the underwear she had been wearing for the hundreds of years she had been alive and living in the woods, and threw them to the ground. The underwear hissed in the sunlight, they were stained, browned like tea and covered with patches of blue-green lichen like mold. The UV rays were reacting with the potent chemicals that had become embedded in the cotton fabric overtime, both through wear and magic.

The witch approached her new underwear. This underwear was the man and she lifted the pair up to her face to admire her workmanship. A pair of white cotton bikini cut briefs with a small white bow in front on the elastic. She put them on and set her skirt back over her body. They felt good on her.

The man would be fated to hundreds of years of being farted on, totally aware the whole time, unable to eat or sleep or relax or never not be able to smell. The witch sighed with content, and carried on with her day. She approached her bike, threw her legs over it, and took off in another direction, possibly to go harvest some wild herbs for tea or maybe something else. Her underwear rubbed against the seat and this pushed the acidic sweat dripping down her body into the cotton. It had begun. Always be happy for others' luck and do not try to take it away.

Sometimes you sexually assault yourself

My message to Carrie Bradshaw is your thoughts
are your enemy

I'm allowed to make up words to songs
Like if I hear them on the radio and they're stuck
in my head and I don't really remember the words
Or it sounds like something else and I mishear it
I'm allowed to make up words

Contrary to popular narratives and tropes I actually think I was born into this life as a human and not as a bug as punishment for my past lives. If you were a bad person why would God reincarnate you as a bug? To be a human is ultimately the most an animal can possibly suffer on this planet. Humans spend their entire lives trying to have what bugs have. You have a forty-dollar co-pay for mindfulness training so maybe one day your mind can come close to the lack of existential back-and-forth an insect has

You know when you're watching TV and it induces psychosis in you? Like you keep watching episodes of the same thing and that reality starts to outweigh the amount of your reality you experience in your real life and you start thinking of your life as only taking place in the locations on the show? And like, how limiting that is? You're like, these are my friends. This is what I do. This is what I eat. These are our conflicts and resolutions. I love my cast and crew.

Writing Prompt #1

Finish this sentence! Explain why using at least 5-8 complete sentences

My nemesis is . . .

_____

_____

_____

_____

_____

_____

_____

_____

The same people who say you must buy something to use our bathroom are the same people
who say why does the street always smell like pee

When you live somewhere it never rains it feels
very serious to puke on the sidewalk

Dreams come to life and die everyday, often
times both in the same day

My body sucks so I make the fool's choice and
punish it

How unfair it is to never be able to be unreal

When you teach someone how to do something,
sometimes they know it forever even if it isn't
important or helpful which is something to think
about before giving out lessons

The second time me and my new boyfriend met he asked me if I'd rather be an elephant or a dolphin. I said, "Elephant. I don't like dolphins."

I am averse to the way they are aggressively horny and smart and conniving although I respect it. I just find it to be very powerful and scary so I must look away.

He says to me, "I'd be a dolphin. I love dolphins."

Months later I watched a YouTube video on "Homosexuality In Nature" by a person on YouTube named TREY the Explainer. He talks about gay animal behavior. On the screen, split with each animal on one side, is a photograph of an elephant and a dolphin. TREY the Explainer goes on to say that both dolphins and elephants generally only mingle sexes briefly during mating season. During the rest of the year the animals separate by male and female and form same-sex partnerships and have sex, hunt together, and live together exclusively. It's more common in males, but females do it too. They continue these relationships for years, only meeting up to breed.

We broke up so I never got to see a dolphin and an elephant fuck.

When I was eleven I got in a terrible accident.

When I was five my parents got a dog. His name was Maximillian, never Max. I had seen the name written somewhere once and thought it was beautiful. Probably saw it on a bookend somewhere, or on TV.

I later learned he was named after a Hapsburg, Maximilian I, who ruled as both the King of Romans (with his father) and then eventually Holy Roman Emperor from 1486 until he died in 1519. Maximilian I's father Frederick III named him after Saint Maximilian of Tebessa who, in the year 295, when brought out in front of a senator refused to be a soldier for the emperor and go to war at the age of twenty-one. He was then beheaded. Frederick III named his son Maximilian because he is said to have seen Saint Maximilian of Tebessa come to him in a dream once and warn him of danger.

Maximilian I's mother died when he was young. She was Eleanor of Portugal. When Maximilian I was seventeen, unlike Saint Maximilian, he commanded his first military campaign, although it is reported he received help from more experienced generals too. This was against Hungary. In August of the next year he was married. He did many things after that but I am not too interested in them. They are not important to this story.

In 1501 Maximilian I fell from his horse and permanently injured his leg, causing him chronic pain for the rest of his life. From 1514 everywhere he traveled he took his coffin just in case he died. In 1518 he saw an eclipse and thought he was surely going to die. He went back to Innsbruck, which was the capital of Austria during his rule, and innkeepers refused him. He was always spending outside of his means, and in the end was refused any more lines of credit despite his royal status. He then had a stroke and died a few months later, just after the new year.

This is all according to his Wikipedia page.

—

Maximilian, my dog, was and is beautiful. He is a small, white toy poodle. In my earliest memories he is running fast in circles over green grass, he appears to be hovering almost. We were children and free together. It was a time I will never forget.

I was eleven. I had just begun to sit in the front seat of the car. It was a very big deal for me. I was big enough, adult enough, tall enough, old enough. I needed something outside me to tell me those things, to mirror the excitement I had inside to one day be a woman. To be able to make my own decisions and run my adult life. When you're a child you want to be grown so bad. Now I know not to rush.

Maximilian was so sweet in the car. He rode great, never drooled or got too sick. Never paced or pooped or cried. Just sat. He was on my lap, like always. Kind of to the side looking at the window, but he was on me like a baby lamb. His hair was matted because we never brushed it. We then always had to shave him. I know now that is bad, but as a child the texture of his hair made me so happy to feel. I remember closing my eyes. It was a warm summer day. I could see the sun shine through my eyelids and make me able to see the amber color of the inside of my eye skin. I thought to myself, "Where does this color come from?

When you close your eyes, why is it sometimes black and sometimes orange? And sometimes fireworks? When you close your eyes really tight, why do you sometimes see fireworks?" The radio played low and I could only hear the changing of the sounds of the tone of the talking but not the words themselves. The air was hot and stale. My father was driving. He was not speaking. I did not feel particularly close to my father. I couldn't remember where my mother was. At home I guess. You always end up remembering very insignificant things about important life events.

My father did not stop at a red light. I'm not sure why. Humans make mistakes. He blew right through it, at an intersection we had been going through my whole life. Two intersections away from our house. Statistically it is actually pretty probable. It is probable to get into an accident like this, statistically. Near your home and stuff. Traffic accident statistics are pretty alarming if you look at them. You'll learn a lot. Research helps me understand what happens to me and why.

My father ran the red light and I remember looking and seeing a car headed for me, from the passenger window. A four-door forest green sedan. There was no time to say anything. I looked down at Maximilian and saw his beautiful brown eyes and then it was dark for a while. I woke up later. I was eleven so I don't remember everything so bare with me. I was in the hospital. I was in so much pain. I was very scared and many things were attached to me, in the hospital, in the hospital bed. I found out later that I woke up a week after. I was in the dark for a week. I didn't know what they did to me until a few days after I woke up.

—

I hold a reminder for this accident everyday, on my body. Maximilian was hit by the airbag on impact, which then hit me. It happened so fast though, and we were hit together, really. I was only eleven like I said, and actually much later found out I was not supposed to be in the passenger seat, really. My father was neglectful at best. A tyrant at worst. I was too short and too young and it put me in danger. It doesn't matter much about him. This story is not about them, my parents. My mother and father both died when

I was eighteen. My father died crashing his car drunk. The car he got after this accident and had until he died. He totaled his other car when the person hit us. He drove it as fast as he could off a small wooden bridge. Kinda like in the movie *Beetlejuice*, starring Alec Baldwin and Geena Davis and Michael Keaton and Winona Ryder, directed by Tim Burton. I believe it was the guilt. My mother died shortly after of what I believe to be a broken heart. Not for my father, for me. For all of it. I don't remember much of it. That's a convenient thing for a storyteller to say about a difficult emotional state to articulate: "I don't remember!" But, I really don't.

Maximilian's bones jutted through my soft tissue, changing the composition of my body forever. And his. It is specific to us and our story. The way he was sitting, like a lamb, his folded legs somehow found their way through parts of my chest and lower abdomen.

His two front legs: his right went through my right lung and his left went through somewhere under my ribcage. His head resting on my right arm near my armpit, with his eyes pointed downward.

His back legs went through my digestive sys-
tem. His back right leg went through me near my
stomach and his back left leg somewhere near
my colon. I can't remember because they fixed it
all or at least settled it in a way I can't see exactly
so I don't remember. He impaled me with himself
from the impact of the airbag, diagonal through the
entire front of my body. It was like he stepped leg-
high in mud and couldn't get out and the mud was
actually all my most important organs. The only
way to save me was to keep Maximilian, essentially.
Technology is really good now. If you do research
you'll understand how they did it.

If you Google my name you can read all about me.
I've been on the news, on *Oprah.* On all types of
talk shows. I am young in all of the videos. I am
about twelve or thirteen. It was a short-lived stint in
the public eye. My parents took the cash and then
we disappeared. I have none of it now obviously,
but that's why I went on those shows then. Sort of
like Octomom or some other tabloid freak. I hope
one day they make a statue of me at a Ripley's
Believe It or Not! Museum. You can listen to inter-
views with the doctors explaining this insane surgery that changed the way humans look at life

forever. There's an episode of *60 Minutes* about it. There's a *Saturday Night Live* skit. That's me.

The part everyone was interested in is that Maximilian fused to my body in the accident. They couldn't remove his legs or it would kill me. Maximilian also did not die from the airbag. The force did not kill him. It was a miracle. We were a miracle together. He seemed unwounded despite being hit at such a fast and intense rate by the airbag. Bizarrely though, like through divine pro- tection, Maximilian and I became one. He no longer pooped. He pooped through me. From my butt. The doctors did that to us. Even if I fed him applesauce with a spoon he pooped from my butt. We peed the same pee. We had the same heart. He pumped my blood. Our blood. He saw with his eyes though. He tasted with his tongue and thought with his brain. He didn't have access to my mind and I didn't have access to his. In the surgery they attached his entire body to me. They finished the job. They didn't really know what to do, this had never happened to anyone before. The dog and the person both live. So they did their best to leave us alive the way we were. My skin overlapped his body. Our tissues connected and healed together. The fur faded into my skin and skin faded into fur.

I remember when I woke up he was still asleep with his own tubes in a person hospital. Because he was now a person too in the way that I was also a dog. I thought he was just laying on me. I was a little girl high on pain pills.

The doctors walked us all the way through the cave to get to the other side. All the way into the darkness to get to the light. They told me Maximilian would live as long as I lived and vice versa. I was ok with this.

—

My dog lived in my body, on my chest. We were one. We did everything together because there was no choice. We gestured together. Followed inquiries together. Shared hobbies. I was pulled from public school and isolated to protect me from judgment. Not sure what I'd have done if it was my child. I didn't even care. I felt like I had a gift. After the accident everyone around me began to protect me. I really respect that, the effort required. The lengths to keep my self esteem. I wasn't allowed to look at what people said about me. I went on TV shows but because I was a child, the live studio audiences did not leer at me. I think they also saw how much I loved my dog. And because being disgusted openly and publicly would be wrong. At a child especially.

I lived somewhere fairly small where everyone knew me and respected us enough and everything we had been through to not hurl insults at me. Because I was homeschooled I avoided being bullied, although I always felt left out socially. I compensated academically and by throwing myself into other interests and attaching myself to the mythology of my life. I can't believe I was chosen. I'm so special.

I applied to college my senior year of high school. I was homeschooled still. With my incredibly niche and tragic story I could go to any college in the country. My resume included being on *Oprah*, like I said. And everywhere I went I brought my dog with me. Because I was also my dog. Sometimes people would say, "Excuse me ma'am! You can't have a dog in here! Even if you smuggle it in your shirt!" like at the movies or something and I'd say "Oh actually

he is attached to me. We share the same body. I
can show you or show you a news article about
it to prove it. His name is Maximilian." I am well-
accomplished. Like I said, I could go to any college.

—

I am now twenty-seven years old. I turn twenty-eight after the new year. I type into Google
"dangers of driving with your dog on your lap."
I type the whole sentence knowing some of
the words are extra and not needed, like "of." It
is what I do when I feel bad and want to make
myself feel worse. I am sure everyone here is
familiar with looking at things on the internet that
hurt you because it is better than feeling nothing.
This article on NWFdailynews says

Beyond potentially causing accidents, there are
very real dangers to allowing a pet to sit on your
lap. If a crash did occur, a small pet could easily
be crushed by a deployed airbag, or thrown from
the car and injured or even killed. In addition, an
unrestrained dog can act as a missile during a
crash. AAA notes that an unrestrained 10-pound
dog, where the vehicle is only traveling at 30

mph, will exert roughly 300 pounds of pressure in a crash! So, imagine the devastation that can cause to your pet and anyone in his path.

It is funny because the website doesn't know I don't have to imagine it. Another site called theglobeandmail.com which I believe is a Canadian publication says:

> While I refer to the airbag as having a pillow-like effect, that is only because it is designed to deflate as quickly as it inflates - shrinking a millisecond after it has reached maximum size and contact has been made with it. Until that moment, the bag is inflating at high speed. Anything in the way will be hit with massive force more powerful than the biggest, most powerful heavyweight boxer's punch.

These are all clickbait articles on websites that primarily exist so people will click on boner pill ads.

I went to a very accomplished college. I graduated. I work in my field. I give motivational talks sometimes at conferences, make appearances on my academic research. I want to go to grad school soon. I'd like to become a teacher. I love to study and learn and grow. Maximilian is still here. He is older, but he is mostly the same. We sleep together every night obviously. I lay on my back and our breaths sync up. It's cool though because he doesn't need to go on walks or anything. We shower together. We do everything together.

My story actually begins now. The part I want to focus on and tell you. That was a lot of backstory to understand what I have gone through to get me where I am today. I am realizing a lot of things just now as an adult. There's a lot of parts of life I didn't get to live because Maximilian lives in me. I never felt a loss before, but as I settle into my own adulthood I begin to wonder and fantasize that maybe I missed out.

I have never kissed anyone or had sex. I have never done anything above the pants or under them. My breast tissue has grown severely irregularly, to account for the dog shape. Sometimes I masturbate when Maximilian is asleep. He doesn't know or notice because he is a dog. He doesn't have the same constructions about sex that I have anyway, and he also was fixed before we were fused. I have a lumpy but good butt. Nice legs I think. The delicate arms of a lady and great hands and a warm smile and nice eyes and a positive attitude given everything I've been through. And like I said, I'm very accomplished. I'm the total package. Such a total package that I come with a dog! Ha! I'm kidding. I mean it's true, but I know that's actually the most difficult part of me for someone to love.

At college, I remember the first time I realized I was very scary. Very frightening and grotesque. I accept my truth, but it is shocking. I did not go to parties often because Maximilian does not like loud noises, they aren't good for dogs and they aren't good for babies. I avoided people naturally, because it was what I was taught by my parents after the accident. It kept me safe. You can't always promise safety though, in any form.

I remember a boy walked by and said, "nice dog chest dog girl! You look like a dog too!! WOOF WOOF!" and started barking at me. It broke some sort of silence of lack of acknowledge-ment everyone felt they were suffering from and people laughed and laughed like laughter had been banned for years and was just now done being prohibited. The funny part is Maximilian barked back.

The shame only began once I realized there was something missing because of my difference that I had not been aware of before. Not necessarily love, I felt no lack of love in my life. Maximilian was my best friend, I was never alone. I had my story to keep me alive. But to have my body desired sexually. Be a conquest for a beautiful, smart, strong man who felt compelled to have me and make me his. I felt I would never have this. That I'd die having everything else but this. I put all the pieces together from my past and they all pointed to this.

I'm a grown woman. I have really fostered my own vision. I live by my own approval. When I was eleven years old my dog was surgically attached to my chest because of a tragic accident. My parents died when I was young, although they disappeared mentally and emotionally years before because of their own illnesses and ailments. I did everything with Maximilian. I got myself into school and worked and was respected. I wanted to have

my pussy licked by a man's mouth. I deserved
to feel that much, especially after everything
although I try not to think like that too much.

—

I decided that based on TV and movies my only
option was to hire a male gigolo. Except it's really
hard to find that. It isn't 1980 in Times Square
anymore, so it turns out that was kind of a fan-
tasy. They are all gay too mostly, it seems. I
would let a gay man lick my pussy too but I don't
know, this is just the way everything unfolded.
Accidents happen. The only person I could find to
lick my pussy was a beautiful woman and I found
her by accident.

Jessica was absolutely beautiful. The most beautiful woman I had ever seen. Maybe the only
beautiful woman I had ever really seen. I never
looked before and now I noticed. When I first saw
her I didn't know her name at all, I found it out
later. We met by chance. I never really met people
besides work or school colleagues that I had pro-
fessional, removed relationships with, on account
of not getting out much. Maximilian was my

deepest and closest bond, man's best friend and family. In public I often protect myself, by making it appear my dog is not part of my body but that he's just in a sling. That's my mechanism.

Jessica was standing outside Wegman's. This is a regional, local grocery chain. There is one where I live. I had not seen her in the store at all. I needed to get a head of broccoli and toilet bowl cleaner. I didn't even see her as I left, like walking out of the store. I only saw her once I was in my car, driving from the parking lot to the exit. We locked eyes. Hers were blue like a gray blue and sort of worried but also like she knew a joke nobody else knew. As someone who has many jokes inside them too at all times I understood this. Like seeing the sun for the first time after a lifetime underground.

Jessica slowly approached the driver's side window of my car. She asked, like she asks this all the time to people, "Can I get a ride?" and I said sure. Seems ironic that I said "It's not 1980" earlier because I couldn't get a male escort but now I'm picking up a hitchhiker. Pretty old school. Maximilian peaked his head and turned, sort of sticking out of the hole I cut for his head or make in any of the shirts of sweaters I wear unless it is one I use specifically for hiding him. He was gesturing like a dog at her, wanting to smell her, curious as to why she was here and who she was.

She was wearing an outfit that upon closer inspection that sort of looked like a costume. She had a vest with patches sewn on to it, maybe to look punk? But it wasn't weathered through time or wear, so she definitely just made it. Like this was a new phase. She had boots and tights and a skirt and a cropped black t-shirt on. Her hair was long and brown but the type of brown hair someone has if they were blonde as a child. Like very light brown. And they'll really cling to that blonde identity too. They're always convinced of their blonde in present day too. Childhood can really impact people.

I said, "Where do you want to go?" and she said, "I actually hadn't thought that far yet. I just want to leave right here right now." So I said ok and I drove us back to my house like we had been living there together for twenty-five years. On the drive it was mostly silent. She pet Maximilian and I drove with all my attention because I like to drive safely and carefully given everything I have been through.

We pulled into the driveway and I put my car in park. I got out and grabbed my bag and Jessica followed quite comfortably.

"Damn, so you never put that dog down, huh?"

I can respond to this easily. I don't find it offensive.

"Oh, actually, I got in a terrible accident as a child. He is fused to my chest. We have the same body."

Jessica's eyes widened and she sat in silence for a second. Probably to process the fact that the dog she touched was attached to my body. Oftentimes people need time to repress their desire to ask me to show them me naked, what we look like together. But her aesthetic sensibilities let me know she favored the macabre or whatever, and could probably process the strange.

In a fight my parents got in before they both died, and maybe one of my only memories of him I remember, my drunk father, slurring his words, said "Be careful of anyone who wants to fuck a dog." Completely inappropriate to say to me or any child, but I didn't know what this meant for a long time. Until after he died. My mother slurred back, agitated and sharp and tight and at the end of her rope, not from alcohol but from crying, "For the love of GOD how often do you go around meeting DOG FUCKERS?????????"

—

"When I touch him do you feel it?" she said, petting the top of his head.

"No."

"Oh. ok. Because that would be weird."

"Yea it would."

"Does he feel when you are touched?"

"I'm not sure but I don't think so. He has never been hurt when I am hurt."

"What do you mean you're not sure? Wouldn't you just know?"

"No, he's a dog. So he can't talk and tell me."

"True," she laughed.

"I have something to ask you. How old are you?"

"I'm twenty-four."

"Ok, cool, so I am twenty-seven. I turn twenty-eight in the new year. I have never been touched or kissed by anyone before. I don't want to assume too much about you. But I have $800 in cash right now. In an envelope. I have been trying to find someone to kiss and touch me for the first time. So I can die knowing what it feels like. Do you know? Do you know what this feels like for me? I want my pussy licked. Have you ever had your pussy licked? I have seen it in photos and movies and I touch myself and think about it and I think it is my time too. You're very beautiful. As you can see, it is very hard for me to find someone. I am a professional woman. I am well respected. You can Google me."

Jessica said nothing. She looked at my eyes then looked down into Maximilian's in which he understood nothing of what was happening or cared, then she looked back at me and back at my house and back to the car and to the road and then back at me. She opened and closed her mouth a few times, like she was getting ready to say something and nothing could come out.

She looked at me and she smiled a little and we went inside. This answer was yes. I am clean and well-kept. And I felt I was offering a fair amount of money, and quite kind. And anyone could have seen that this very sad grown woman with a dog in her needed what everyone else needs.

She asked me where my bedroom was and I pointed at it and she led me inside, into my own bed. She told me to lay on it so I did. She took off my shoes and socks. She took off my pants, wiggled them around my ankles and over my feet and left them on the floor.

I was in my underwear and my shirt and she stared up at me. I could tell she didn't know how to pro-ceed. This was uncharted territory for both of us.

I finally broke the silence, "I will put a blanket over Maximilian."

I grabbed a throw and put it over the top half of my body, exposing my legs as well as my face.

"Would you like to kiss?"

And before I could answer there was a mouth over me, from above. On my mouth. Moving at a rhythm I've never felt before. It made my whole body warm and loose. Her tongue tasted like someone else's life I never lived and we kissed for I think maybe two minutes actually but it felt like forty-five because it had never happened before. I was glad that was off the list.

She moved to my legs again. This whole time I'm laying on the bed and she's working around Maximilian, pretending the entire top half of my body is a void. There is no body. I liked this option the best too. She made me feel comfortable. Jessica was the first and only other person to ever see my under-wear, see me naked. She took my underwear off, and the air on my genitals surged. The air around me felt electric and static and sensitive to a new wavelength I could not see or understand before. I moaned involuntarily. Jessica put my clitoris in her mouth, and sucked. She tasted my wetness. I had never done any of this before. I am twenty-seven years old. I turn twenty-eight in the new year. I came all over her. It also probably took two minutes. I completely forgot about my body, and everything that made me me. For a brief second I understood why I longed for this so bad and why I felt its absence.

—

Quickly, the room came back and I felt normal. I moved the blanket over the top of my body to the bottom half of my body, over my exposed and sensitive genitals and away from Maximilian. Maximilian was no different. In his world, through his eyes, nothing had happened. Nothing had changed. He was just under a blanket for a few minutes, sleeping anyway, because he is tired and old these days and can't even walk anyway. When I lifted the blanket up he only opened one eye to look at me, like a giant squid through a porthole, and immediately closed it after.

He felt no different, but I did. Jessica was so nice and so beautiful. The nicest woman I ever met. For many reasons. She asked me where the money was. I gave it to her in the envelope, like I promised. She said, "Ok I'm going to walk now."

"Walk where?"

"I actually hadn't thought that far yet. I just want to leave right here right now."

"Ok, it was nice meeting you."

"It was nice meeting you too."

She shut the door behind her, and we crawled into bed. Me and Maximilian. He came with me because he has to. He is attached to me so he goes where I go.

It was the longest and best I had slept since I was eleven years old. I dreamed I was running so fast down the street, it was like a drone was shooting a video of me, it was from that point of view. And I was running so fast it looked like I was hovering.

It is time to hike. I hike semi-frequently. Have a pair of worn hiking boots from the thrift store. I look up moderate trails on Alltrails and track my steps and miles and consider it a hobby of mine. It definitely occupies a good portion of my free time. I go to my favorite trail. It's a ridge trail, running parallel to the cliffed mountain. Rocky, semi alpine. There's pine trees, needles on the floor. As well as hardwoods though. Rattlesnake plantain orchid leaves that stay all year round. Large patches of green moss. I park my jeep at the trailhead, leaving behind everything except my car keys and a small digital camera and my Camelbak filled with water and begin my descent. It's a small five mile loop. It will be nice and easy and relaxing.

It rained a few days ago. I forgot because today is the first real sunny, dry day. But, the trails have not become dry yet. It is muddy. I am navigating the rocks, they are slick and wet and placed in between the patches of mud. I think nothing of this really other than in an observational way. I walked for a while with no incident. I stop at certain views to take photos. I take a photograph of myself in front of a view. I walk. I walk until I slip. I slipped on a cliff, where the trail is small. I was probably three to four miles in. Sort of being less careful about my footing. Daydreaming. I slip and fall like a nightmare. I slip off a cliff. First I land on a large boulder directly under the cliff, under the cliff directly before the larger drop. I am filled with rage and the feeling of boiling and nothing and agony and my vision is going in and out because there is some part of my body in pain in a way I cannot even see or recognize. I don't know what happened to me. What popped or changed or moved. I was just electric inside with pain and terror and fear and regret and shame. My body shifted more. It acted for itself, which plunged me off the boulder, tumbling down the cliff more. I guess I couldn't keep my footing? My grip? I didn't know where my feet or my hands were because the pain was everywhere and I could distinguish the feeling in my limbs. I fell to my final spot. I felt pine needles on my face. I felt leaves. I think I was face down in the dirt. I don't know how long I was there. I felt softer, lighter. I felt farther away from being on fire. I can't explain it. You wouldn't under-stand. But I felt my face. My face against the pine needles. My mangled limbs. My blood seeping into the ground. My exposed bones. My visible muscles and fat layers. My mangled ass in the air. My mangled hand, contorted. And as life sort of left the rest of me I felt the life go to my cock. The blood stopped pouring out of my body and poured into my cock. And I reached my hand over. I don't know how. Adrenaline. And I began to stroke my cock, which somehow survived. That somehow was stronger after falling. I pumped and I pumped my cock in my hand and I felt lightheaded. I thought about everything I had ever done that got me to be a mangled body on the bottom of a cliff, without an Iphone in my pocket. I came in my hand. That's all I can remember.

You make a monster of someone when you are not honest with them

I like nice people who chew gum
I am not nice and I don't chew gum

Fool me once
Fool me twice

if everything is so deeply touched and tainted by

the structural powers at hand
if you agree every single aspect of our cul-
ture has an insidious disease that creeps into
everything
if everything is spoiled
why would your friends, your desires, your wants,
your needs be free from that?
how could you be so blessed to be the only person with an inner world that isn't tainted by the
outside world?

Every idea I get is an idea for someone else. My ideas are never for me. It is just the purpose of my thoughts, for someone else. I know because I will think of something to do or say and I will think, "hmmm that would be really cool if someone else did that. I still don't know what I will do though. Not sure what to do with that idea or what to do now." Maybe one day I will think of an idea for me

January fool
February fool
March fool
April fool
May fool
June fool
July fool
August fool
September fool
October fool
November fool
December fool
The first of every month

Not scared of living alone only dying alone
The shadow at night is the same shadow every night
It clocks in to work too
I forgive everyone for being crazy but I cannot be
in contact again, sorry

The thing is for a writer I don't have a very good imagination.

They've already written about everything that's happened, other writers.

Shoplifting, drugs, school, love, career, family, road trips, farmland, cities, ice cream, middle school bullies, friends, neglectful parents, saving an animal, killing an animal, rape, assault, academics, school, art, music, fights, cancer, summer, fall, winter, spring, death, being born, divorce, and marriage, being alone and being very much together. The ocean, the woods, sleeping on a mattress on the floor, sleeping in my car, sleeping in a motel, sleeping in my childhood home, sleeping in a hotel, sleeping in a tent, sleeping on a trampoline, sleeping in a mansion. Being sedated and being stimulated.

All has been written before.

One day my mom tells me, "The sad thing about Simon & Garfunkel is as much as they argued they needed each other. Paul Simon can't sing like Art Garfunkel and Art Garfunkel can't write a song like Paul Simon."

My grandfather cannot hear me banging on his door. I am banging on the door because I have to piss so bad. I just got off the bus at his house and he is supposed to let me in but he is watching some Western movie he recorded off TV on a VHS and the volume is so loud because he can not hear so he can not hear me over the cowboys to come let me in. Twenty minutes pass and he finally comes to the door. I don't think he heard me screaming I just think he was just checking to see because he noticed I was late and I happened to be out there. I run inside and go to the bathroom to piss immediately. It is a hot day and I was dancing outside in jeans to keep myself from wetting myself. I remember swinging my backpack around. Afterwards, I sit at his dining room table to do my homework and his house smells like cabbage and he tells me he remembers when broccoli was invented when he was a child. When he was a child and worked on his parents farm he remembers when they came out with broccoli. I have a hard time believing him because just twenty minutes ago he could not hear me banging on his door. I think maybe he is out of touch. I go home and look at the Wikipedia article for broccoli and of course his memory is correct.

My friend says to me you don't have to understand
something to love it
That was almost ten years ago

A religious fast where I give up the comfort of
being miserable
In exchange for silence and nothing
Time goes by quicker when you're older
And you will realize it is better when everything
means less

I thought to myself wow I'm so excited to move into my friend's house. I know they have this piano. Maybe I'll teach myself how to play piano on their piano. I'm always looking to pick up new hobbies to enrich my life and challenge my brain. My friend must have thought to themself, "Wow my friend is moving here! Finally I have an excuse to stop playing the piano because it is very hard and I'm tired from all the work I've been doing on it these past few months. And it takes up too much space in my apartment." So my friend sold it because also the room with the piano in it would be the room I'd be moving into and there isn't a room for a piano and a bed and it couldn't go anywhere else.

It's a book about living. I write every day. I write as me and I write as characters. I make lists of stories I'd like to write but then the lists themselves become the story. And then the stories get intertwined with the truth about my life. And then the story becomes ultimately about a storyteller . . . about being a storyteller. And then you can't tell who is talking. It becomes about the process. It becomes about not separating life from art because I consider the things I think off the top of my head to be my best art. And then the book becomes the diary of someone who likes to tell the truth and lie at the same time because I like to play pretend. But I also like to share personal anecdotes. But then you realize the narrator is sad and pathetic and stupid, but funny. But then you realize the characters are the same way too. But then you also love the stories, real and fake. And they teach you things about yourself and even when it is bad and scary you have things to learn from them.

I don't want to be high the next time we sleep together. Sometimes I think I just compulsively do things to take me farther from my body cuz on a regular day at night that's what I have to do to fall asleep but when I'm with you I want to be present so why would I want to smoke and smoke and drink and drink and leave you there. Two glasses of wine is the perfect place to be.

Good love opens you up. That's actually why it's important because good love gets directly put on you and allows you to keep giving that good love to other people.
You touch me and suddenly it's easier to touch other people even in simple ways like hugging my friend while she cries and rubbing her back or talking to strangers and asking them where they're from it's easier because that love opened me

Guys I just don't wanna get lost in the vast ocean again I think I can swim so good I get out real far in the water and I drown
and as i drown I forget my name I forget my story I forget where I was born
I think I can swim so good everytime.
When I really get to the beach I run as fast as I can. I run into the water and I swim.
I swim
When the birds sing at night I get scared. When they don't sing at night I get scared.
Hundreds of bats living in a chimney like a high-rise apartment building

A few months ago I was sitting at the kitchen table and someone told me

"I took all your words at face value. You told me everyday that you mean what you say. That you hate subtext. That you only say exactly what you mean and don't play games. So I'm confused as to why you'd lie to me the whole time you're saying that. What's it all for? What were you trying to prove?"

I swam into the ocean

It has been 1000 years and I have had many birthdays and many holidays and there is no better gift than forgiveness. It is an ancient medicine.

You know when you're in bed with someone and they are spooning you and you keep sort of pretending you're readjusting and getting comfortable but it's all a ruse so you can rub your butt and their genitals and get them horny so they slip it in you? That's like wrestling in the sense that *WWE Smackdown* or whatever is all choreographed. So even when two men are beating John Cena, I can see little moments where John Cena lifts his leg into the arms of the man who is grabbing him only so he can be thrown over the ring onto the floor in the perfect way. I watch him move his face towards a fist so a punch can land. I watch him grab for the hand that is reaching for him even when he is not supposed to want it

I had finally gotten into the crawl space of my apartment. When I get obsessed with something I really do get quite obsessed so lately it has been about this space in my apartment I can't access.

You know when you're living in a shitty rental and they have those weird aluminum panels some-times that are just like, drilled to the wall? You assume it is something electric, or to cover up a hole, or a chimney or something a normal civilian wouldn't understand. Something only a landlord could understand.

I got real obsessed with the hole in my apartment because i would knock on it and sense a large empty space behind it. I could just tell by the vibration, much like a spider that senses prey.

I thought about it for a long time and watched YouTube videos and stuff, about going into crawl spaces. I watched some videos on caving too for good measure. I bought an outfit to wear made of plastic that would protect me from fiberglass or bat poop. Also a respirator so my lungs wouldn't fill with the same. I was going to open it and go inside and when I was done I would put it back to ensure I got my deposit back. I wasn't trying to ruin the place.

My $30 drill from Wal*Mart was able to screw the panel off easily. It was definitely not an electric panel. I took it off to expose a dark, breathing cage inside of my house. Pretty cool. I shined my flashlight in and it was a relatively finished cave space, exposed brick, not much. I stuck my head in first and looked down in all directions. Up, down, left, right. It went forward. I could fit my body through the tight hole and shimmy my way in, but I was afraid I wouldn't be able to turn around and maybe suffocate and die because nobody knew I was in here. I heard about people who died in caves this way, from the videos I watched. And this is a cave of sorts, to me.

I started to regret opening this space. Not from fear, but for some other reason. Someone had been here not that long ago before me and it took away something from the experience for me. The person here before seemed stupid and lost and I wasn't either of those things. It was bringing down my energy and excitement. I didn't feel like an explorer anymore. All of a sudden I felt so sad that I wanted to kill myself. For some reason I started to think about my family and all the things nobody ever said and I was filled with homesickness for nothing. You know how it is.

But, because of my disappointment, I was now free from my obsession. I shimmied backwards out. I drilled the panel back on. I took off my suit and respirator. I threw them away. I moved on to the next thing.

They say admitting you have a problem is the hardest part so now i'm like ok when do the easier parts start?

I took it for granted and lost my ability to "find beauty in the mundane" probably because I bragged about how good I was at that for too many years.

When you say, "I'm saving this for a special occasion" I think to myself, "what is more special than every day?"

The group of people who self identify with being perverts or strange. What if they're not strange or perverts at all? They have to be, because even if they are lying it is very strange and perverted to lie like that. To lie about being perverted is a type of perversion.

The worst feeling in the entire world is going to bed and thinking to yourself, "I will be a better person tomorrow. Tomorrow I will finally be a good person."

My father was a member of a fraternity. And I'm
going to rush into my father's frat. I feel nothing,
really. I guess I worked hard to be where I'm at.
I think all the smartest people in the world recognize the fact that anyone can get anywhere
with the right support, and of course I can exer-
cise my nepotism whenever. So the combination
of supportive parents and my parents being
who they are made it so I got into whatever Ivy
League school I wanted to. So I'm here. And I
don't care. Not in this like, "Oh, I don't care, I'm
going to fail on purpose" kind of way, but just like,
what mistake would I have to make to ruin my
life forever? It would be hard to really throw it all
away. People like me are afforded many chances.
I read. I write. I consider myself comparatively
sensitive, at least to my peers. I'm a soft and car-
ing lover, for a young man of my kind.

In my AP Sociology class in high school,
before I even got to college we read a paper
on frat hazing. I was particularly interested
because it is part of my lineage and heritage.
It talked about the effects of people bonding
this way. Why frat hazing still happens, etc. It's
been proven that groups bond through trauma.
That happens whether or not the trauma is on

purpose. Hazing is on purpose, planned, but some group trauma isn't. I don't have much experience with that kind of group trauma though, except hating school collectively with my peers. My peers who also resent their parents and their lives. Even primates when faced with a collective trauma grow closer afterwards and respect their leaders more. This speaks to the experience of frat hazing but also what does it say about the American nuclear family? Or the workplace? Lol? I wrote about it in my final paper for that class and I got a four on the AP test without studying too much. I told you I read and write.

Anyway in this study, the study that said groups bonded through trauma, they asked fraternity and sorority students to discuss their experiences. Members of these groups tended to have positive associations with the hazing behaviors they partook in that featured "social deviance." I am a fan of social deviance because I love masturbation and things of that nature. The study showed hazing exists to increase the social dependency you have on the groups that haze you. It makes you want to continue to be around those who hazed you. It makes everyone feel stronger together. The study went on to just talk about attachment the-ory in general. I guess at one point "for science" they even got a bunch of puppies and raised them and raised half of them good and half of them bad and in the end the ones who were treated worse were actually more attached and looking for approval from the owners than the group who was treated right. I feel this way with my dad a lot. I want him to like me so much because I am a puppy he raised bad.

Later on, they electrocuted groups of humans. One group was electrocuted harder than the other. And the group that was electrocuted harder felt more connected to their group and found those who got electrocuted heavily to be more attractive than the members who got less electrocuted. Scientists attribute this to dissonance theory, where participants over-compensate to deal with their pain by adding more importance to the group. "It is ok I did this because it was for the group," so then they love the group more, they place more importance with the group, or they think that it was all worth it because now they're in this group. Basically, men love being embarrassed if it means they get to join a secret group and have power.

Basically, I'm self-aware but I have to do this anyway because my dad was in a frat. It is like I am being married off for a dowry. It is a non-choice. It is what I must do so my parents continue to pay for school. I'm interested in the social deviance aspect of it all, I guess. So my resistance isn't that strong. I don't care how others perceive me, or my choices. I think frats are lame, but that isn't important. I know this is pretty depraved but it is really hot to imagine having secrets with anyone, let alone a group that large. I'm literally just here on this Earth to kill time. Sometimes when I masturbate I imagine being publicly embarrassed.

The process leading up to the hazing isn't really so important for this story. The intricacies of rushing or whatever. The dance and courtship of me meeting everyone and them asking me back. It is quite romantic and delicate compared to what will come after.

Frats make you drink and vomit and do bad things like that. I don't care about those things. During the hazing, those things were fine. I disassociated and crawled on my knees through broken glass and swam in a kiddie pool full of piss and cum and ketchup or whatever. I chugged a whole bottle of malt liquor and jumped off the roof. Whatever. Whatever. Those are all things I'd do in this classic way of like, "Oh what else is going to release chemicals in my brain if I've already had it all?" Like I said, I'm a nihilist. Actually, I don't think I said that yet. But I know you sort of caught that subtext and tone.

I don't necessarily remember the linear movement of time during these weeks. We were not on a normal sleep schedule and everyday was like, jokingly torturous. Like hypermasculine summer camp.

One night they asked us all to go into the basement. They had the line of all fifteen of us, naked on our knees. They started on the right side of the line. I was the second from the left. It started out how it kind of always normally started out. They started spanking some dude. I was like cool, we're all gonna get spanked on our knees. What else comes after bathing in cum and ketchup? Vomiting up cheap liquor? The depravity had to continue to be leveled up. I could hear this guy's quiet yelps while I just stared ahead and thought about all the things I had to do this week. I hadn't done laundry in about three weeks, which I considered to be pretty unacceptable. I had to drop off dry cleaning also. Some of my shirts can't go in the machines on campus.

The upperclassman spanking the guy said, "We're going to switch it up now . . . now you're going to open up and take this!" and I heard one of the most familiar sounds to me. It was the sound of someone taking someone else's dick in their entire mouth. I remember thinking in my head, "Oh shit LOL!" I didn't want to look over to my right and see it though because I didn't feel like being yelled at quite yet. If I moved I'd draw attention to myself and receive the same punishment worse and faster. I figured whatever was happening, I'd figure it out later. The dude who was just getting spanked was sucking the guy's dick.

Another upperclassman descended down the stairs holding a box and laughing. I could hear his heavy, ugly footsteps. Clunky and ungraceful and greedy. He said, "Hi pledges!!!! I have a surprise for you!!!" Inside of the box was about 15-20 of the most disgusting looking fleshlights I had ever seen. I've had a few, and taking care of them...it's difficult to maintain their integrity. You have to wash them and dry them and corn starch them after use so they don't rot. Silicone can be so finicky. He began to hand them out, told us to start fucking them, on our knees. On the floor of the basement. So we all did. Honestly, the most depraved part of it to me was that we didn't even get any lube. It felt like this fact I could not dissociate from.

The upperclassmen began to move and position us while we were all jerking off into the fleshlights. Someone pushed me over onto my hands, and all fours, with my butt into the air. They had me bend over, while fucking the fleshlight. They positioned another person being hazed behind me, also fucking a fleshlight. They laughed and pointed! "It's like you two are fucking each other! Ha ha!" Like I said before though, I'm self-aware so therefore not afraid of some dudes calling me gay because I know two years ago when they pledged they had to do the same thing. I'm in my head like, "Ok but you guys fucked each other in the ass too. And now you're family."

I hadn't even looked back until the upperclassman yelled, "You guys should all fuck each other for real now!!" Still, no lube. I looked back because I always wanna know who is about to fuck me. It was Connor. Connor was nice. We met on the first day that we both decided to do this. He had brown hair and green eyes and slightly olive tinted skin and a really tan neck and really tan arms. Like you could tell what shirts he'd wear and how long he'd be in the sun and how he never put sunscreen on. He didn't talk much but also that means he never complained or was annoying. He had a deep, but soft voice. I looked back and he looked at me and honestly in that moment I was like, "Oh, this is chill." It seemed like this was the best case scenario of this worst case scenario. I kind of was like, "Oh he'll take care of me." I let out a secret half smile and he did the same thing. Behind this moment was the insistence of the upperclassman, "Fuck him!!" to everyone and everything. Connor leaned forward, spit on my asshole, and inserted his dick inside me. I remember thinking, how sweet of him to spit in my asshole. Mostly because I didn't hear a single other person spit on anyone else's asshole (a bunch of amateurs in my opinion) but also because I knew it made us look gay for him to do that. And it was nice of him to put that aside to ensure I'd get hurt less than I was inevitably going to.

I dissociated at first. I didn't want to be fucked in the ass necessarily. I also didn't not want to either. I had enjoyed so many splendors in life, tried everything once, so why not this? The Greeks and Romans did this, or whatever. My immediate fight or flight response was to just pretend it wasn't happening, as that is easier to cope with and also my body's classic response as I have learned through the years. I thought about my favorite tree at my mom's house. I thought about what I'd make for breakfast tomorrow. I thought about what I was going to do tonight after this. After about five minutes though the pain turned into a general warmth that took over my body and I kind of thought to myself, "Damn though, Connor is really out here fucking me." The room smelled so fucking bad. Like thirty sweaty balls on unshowered, food-covered new men. It felt and looked like being in a Saw trap from the movie franchise *Saw*. My sweaty knees were sliding and being cut a little on the unfinished floor. You know? It felt like tetanus there.

I turned again, to look at Connor, and saw his forehead sweating. His eyes were closed. He was thrusting at a consistent rhythm, which was also impressive. He honestly looked so fucking beautiful. I'm not insecure so I don't give a shit about saying that. I noticed the mole below his right eye for the first time? I liked the way his skin felt hitting up against my ass? I don't know? Like I said, there was a feeling of warmth all over my body.

The upperclassman took notice. They yelled at Connor, "Fuck him!!!!! Fuck him bro!!!!!!!" and then another upperclassman laughed and said to Connor, "Damn dude! You like this shit?? You gay bro?" but Connor still didn't open his eyes or say anything or make any noise except just his breathing. He was in a trance-like state in my ass. I couldn't help it but I started throwing my ass over Connor's cock. I was like, "Damn they're about to not let me into this frat because I'm sup-posed to be demoralized by this, my dad is going to be so mad." The upperclassman noticed I love it too and started yelling, "Damn dude!!!!!! You like this shit too!!!! You're both gay!!! Take this shit bro!!!" and honestly, I did. I took it. I bet they had never seen real gay sex at their hazing before. Actually, there is no way that is true. These fag-gots love being gay too. It is all a lie. Connor let out a small moan. I didn't let out a single noise the entire time. That was too much. The upper-classman asked Connor if he was going to cum and he said nothing but I felt Connor remove himself from me and then shortly after cum all over my back. After that I felt like it was safe to look around the room. Connor was free from his trance. The warmth all over my body faded away but sort of lingered too. It rested in my arms and legs and made them feel heavy. My ass throbbed and ached. Everyone else was "done" by then, whatever that meant to them. I didn't notice what anyone else was doing the whole time because I felt if I looked, it would complicate my life and I can never ask so I'll never know, but nobody else was fucking by the time we finished. Did they like it? Were they cummed inside of? On top of? Next to? I don't know.

The upperclassman said, "Ok that's enough for tonight actually. See you tomorrow, pledges." I went home and Skyped with my girlfriend that I've been dating since I was fifteen that I forgot to mention at all until right now and ate two Hot Pockets I microwaved and went to bed.

My stupidity is like a curse I put on myself

He doesn't feel like he's lying because he
believes himself

If you're trying so hard to be A good boy all the time
Maybe it's just not in the cards
But you can still relax and have fun
You kno?

Most poppers on the American market are fake. When I go places, talk to gay people, not many of them seem to know this. I know because I work in the poppers industry. Yep, I manufacture and sell poppers. When someone asks me if I want poppers and they're counterfeit I don't know how to tell them. I don't want to sound like a snob, you know? Sometimes it is the worst when someone just rambles on about their job.

There's not that much wrong with counterfeit poppers, they will not kill you. They can be made from random chemicals. Most subreddits and secondhand heresay sources often say they are still made of Isobutyl nitrite, but often diluted with rubbing alcohol, or water, or some other solvent. I have never known them to make anyone deathly ill, or produce worse complications than the ones you can just get from poppers already (I think often of the man who died in the glory hole room of Steamworks in Berkeley supposedly because he did poppers and Viagra at the same time. They sell 100% real poppers in their vending machines there.) The thing is though, you're getting an inferior product for the same price. The counterfeit products require you to inhale them far more, which is worse for you and produces headaches among other negative side effects of poppers.

The counterfeits come "from China," that is what our website (neverfakeit.com) for PWD says. PWD stands for PAC-WEST DISTRIBUTING NV LLC which is the company that manufactures Rush, arguably the most famous poppers in the world. I work for PWD. Our website is a relic of the early internet. It is constructed totally from CSS, it is a scroll of text with hyperlinks that lead to even weirder websites to purchase our products. The fonts go from blue to red, bold, all caps. I can't tell what to read first but I prefer it to the equally complex empty minimalism of like, Apple products. But, I know it contributes to the problem of our consumers not being able to tell which labels are legitimate or not.

The key identifying factor we push for consumers to know is that real PWD poppers do not come with any embossed markings or letters on the sides or bottoms of the bottles. The counterfeits for some reason, if you flip them over, have the raised letters RUSH written on the bottom. You can run your fingers over it like braille and feel the firm glass letters. This is the mark of trickery. I keep scrolling, our website says, "Beginning late FALL 2019 all PAC-WEST DISTRIBUTING NV LLC small PWD® RUSH® BRAND products have 'RUSH' embossed on a RED Cap. All other small PWD® brands have 'PWD USA' embossed on a BLACK cap. All large PWD® brands have a black cap with a PWD® hologram." The website continues, "All of our liquid products are licensed and labeled as SOLVENT CLEANER, not LIQUID INCENSE, not AROMA and not NAIL POLISH REMOVER! Our contents is clearly stated as ISOBUTYL NITRITE, not as ALCOHOL, ACID AND WATER***"

Ironically enough, PWD sued a company called AFAB industries (lol) not that long ago for infringing on our trademark. We reached a settlement agreement in 2016 as we had legal run-ins before, but in 2019, AFAB sued PWD for essentially talking shit about them on their website. PWD claims AFAB Rush is pirated, an inferior product despite our original settlement giving AFAB the right to continue to produce Rush. AFAB argues that PWD can not own our trademarks because how can you trademark an illegal product. Poppers can not be sold for recreation use in the USA, but they can for any commercial purposes covered under the Federal, Drug, and

Cosmetic Act. AFAB claims PWD cannot rely on trademark laws because our product is unlawful. In court they said, "The term 'commercial purpose' means any commercial purpose other than for the production of consumer products containing volatile alkyl nitrites that may be used for inhaling or otherwise introducing volatile alkyl nitrites into the human body for euphoric or physical effects." They go on to say, "'poppers' are recreational drugs inhaled to achieve a high and said to facilitate anal intercourse." AFAB argues that because PWD is aware that our product is sold at "novelty stores" and are "well recognized in the LGBTQ community, they must be used recreationally, and therefore rendered fraudulent and invalid."

We agree to stop fighting. AFAB industrial website has no mention of poppers. With a sleeker, more contemporary design, there is a photo of a man welding on the home page. They manufacture chemicals and equipment, have facilities in China, make chain link fences and extract from botanicals. A quote on the homepage says, "'All truths are easy to understand; the point is to discover them.' – Galileo"

PWD's website still says "***PAC-WEST

DISTRIBUTING NV LLC covenanted not to sue AFAB Industrial Services Inc. for use of the words RUSH, SUPER RUSH, PWD and POWER PACK PELLET or the slogan 'NEVER FAKE IT WITHOUT IT!' (which is not the same as our famous and trademarked slogan 'NEVER FAKE IT!') for Nail Polish Remover goods. AFAB Industrial Services Inc. must place its company name and Bensalem, PA, specifically, 'AFAB Industrial Services Inc. Bensalem PA' on its labels for the aforementioned goods using the words: RUSH, SUPER RUSH, PWD and POWER PACK PELLET. AFAB Industrial Services Inc. is in NO way affiliated with PAC-WEST DISTRIBUTING NV LLC of Nevada and has no ownership interest in PAC-WEST DISTRIBUTING NV LLC or any of its trademarks, trade name and/or trade dress."

What else do you do with a pile of glass except clean it up as best you can and step carefully the next few days in case any pieces you couldn't pick up linger and cut the bottoms of your feet?

No more wanting to be special.

If my view can be molded like clay by someone else I'm like "I have hands too. That means I can shape too."

I need to focus on the positive
My boyfriend found me a toaster oven for free
somewhere on the side of the road
I get my best thinking done at the diner counter
both this and having unprotected sex and driving
without a seatbelt make life interesting

The woman says do you want more coffee it's
nice and fresh I just made it I say sure she pours
me a cup and it tastes burnt

No service the only radio stations that come in
here are country and gospel and AM sportscast-
ers wildly screaming in back-and-forth agony and
bliss depending on what happens
When I'm in the desert I don't drive anymore with
less than a half a tank of gas
I've run out too many times and I refuse to get
stuck again

I'm so fucking hungover. I'm never like this. I don't usually drink so much because I work a lot and it can make work so hard the next day. I am running late. My cat learned how to turn off my alarm recently. When it goes off, he runs over to my iPhone and turns the alarm off on my touch screen. His paw pads can conduct electricity, so he can use a smartphone.

I wake up, get dressed, it is all a blur.

Sometimes you are so tired that you cannot get the sleep from your eyes no matter what you do. You can't even use warm water to wash your face because it is too relaxing. That's where I'm at.

I get into my stupid car that costs a lot of money a month to lease, it is part of why I am so stressed about getting to work. If I don't work I can't pay for my car. If I can't pay for my car I can't go to work. The predicament is as old as time.

It is still dark. It is winter and the sun has not risen yet. I am headed to Starbucks. I actually don't get Starbucks that much. I'm not really that kind of girl. But I needed some-thing, a treat. And if you're already late I am a big believer in just not rushing. If I'm late I'm already late. It is done. If I'm going to be ten minutes late I might as well be an hour late.

They're mostly the same to people, to bosses, I realize over the years.

The Starbucks line is long. I play on my phone. I file my nails with the file I keep in my car. I look at videos and listen to music and text my friends. I order at the little speaker box when I get to it.

"Hi, welcome to Starbucks. How can I help you today?"

"Hi can I get a . . . um . . . grande? Medium? Iced latte. Thanks."

"What kind of milk?"

"Just milk is fine."

"Ok, that will be $5.25, please pull up to the next window."

When I finally get to the window the barista turns to me and says, "The car ahead of you decided to pay it forward."

I pause for a second. "What does that mean?"

"It means they like, bought you your drink. And the people in front of them bought their drink. It has been going on for about seven to eight cars, I suppose. People do it sometimes. Have you ever heard of it? I can tell you how much the car behind you was, so you can see if you want to pay it."

I think for a second, I guess I sort of had? *Pay it forward*? It sounds like some sort of subsidized coffee program . . . I feel overwhelmed by this, and sort of stressed. I feel myself getting confused and annoyed.

"So is my coffee free?"

The barista says yes. She hands me my beautiful iced latte. I am now an hour and a half late for work. The sun is rising. It is cloudy, so it didn't make a clear break over the horizon. But it is clearly day now. The light has shifted. "Do you want to know how much the person behind you paid? So you can continue to pay it forward?"

I look in my rear-view mirror. I see the silhouettes of four bodies in the car. Two in the front and two in the back. Did they order four drinks?

I wanna make it clear, the barista doesn't sound excited. I've never heard anyone speak so neutrally. I think she likes delivering the news just as much as I like hearing it. It must be such a nuisance, as most Starbucks related things generally are.

"Absolutely not. Have a great day."

I pull away. I feel so happy and so ready for the day.

Sex goblin
You wanna live somewhere with no weather
You want to buy your way out of the weather
where it is nice all year long

Sex goblin
You see a dog with the face of a human
It is your worst nightmare come true
A horror you will never forget
It is also the best thing that has ever happened
to you
A horror you will never forget

Sex goblin's mother on the phone says, "I've been
calling for weeks I was wondering if you were ok."
Sex goblin says, "Yea I just work all the time until
late and the time difference makes it hard."
Sex goblins mom says, "I need you to know the
biggest regret in my life is never being or living
alone. I was always married. I've never been
single for more than six months since I was
twenty-three."
Sex goblin says, "Ok . . ."

As a child, I used to stay up all night thinking about the mice in the walls. My mom told me that mice sometimes can chew on the wiring inside the walls of old houses which can start an electrical fire. She said it happens sometimes, to some people, in some places. I stayed up all night waiting for the house to catch on fire. I heard the sound of mice feet in the walls and thought of it as the sound of death. I guess I'd fall asleep at some point, around 3 or 4 a.m. I didn't have stamina. I'd always wake up the next morning wondering how we'd all survive if I wasn't there to think all of our problems away.

Now as an adult I just have control issues and a hard time feeling present, among other things. Not to be overly short but maybe you can relate?

NIGHTBOAT BOOKS

Nightboat Books, a nonprofit organization, seeks to develop audiences for writers whose work resists convention and transcends boundaries. We publish books rich with poignancy, intelligence, and risk. Please visit nightboat.org to learn about our titles and how you can support our future publications.

The following individuals have supported the publication of this book. We thank them for their generosity and commitment to the mission of Nightboat Books:

Kazim Ali • Anonymous (8) • Mary Armantrout • Jean C. Ballantyne • Thomas Ballantyne • Bill Bruns • John Cappetta • V. Shannon Clyne • Ulla Dydo Charitable Fund • Photios Giovanis • Amanda Greenberger • Vandana Khanna • Isaac Klausner Shari Leinwand • Anne Marie Macari • Elizabeth Madans • Martha Melvoin • Caren Motika • Elizabeth Motika • The Leslie Scalapino - O Books Fund • Robin Shanus • Thomas Shardlow • Rebecca Shea • Ira Silverberg • Benjamin Taylor • David Wall • Jerrie Whitfield & Richard Motika • Arden Wohl • Issam Zineh

This book is made possible, in part, by grants from the New York City Department of Cultural Affairs in partnership with the City Council and the New York State Council on the Arts Literature Program.